AND THE TIME MACHINE

ELT

AND THE TIME MACHINE
ELT'S ADVENTURES CONTINUE!

DANIEL R. PARD

authorHOUSE®

AuthorHouse™
1663 Liberty Drive
Bloomington, IN 47403
www.authorhouse.com
Phone: 1-800-839-8640

Published by AuthorHouse 10/15/2014

ISBN: 978-1-4969-4618-8 (sc)
ISBN: 978-1-4969-4617-1 (e)

Library of Congress Control Number: 2014918176

ACKNOWLEDGMENTS

I wish to thank Brad Pard for the map art as well as Elt's website design on eltsadventures.com. In addition, a very special thanks to Heidi Lockridge, who made the novel shine with her magnificent editing performance.

Ralph's Neighborhood

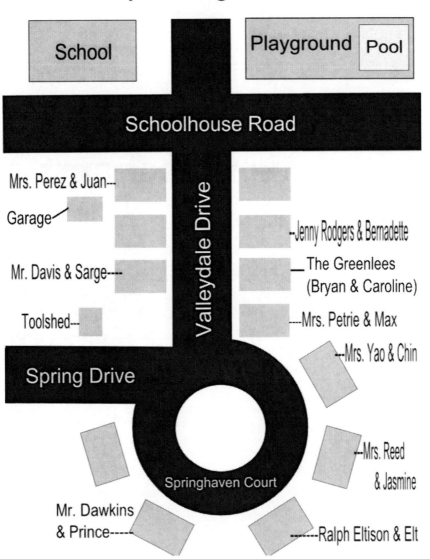

Downtown Spring Valley

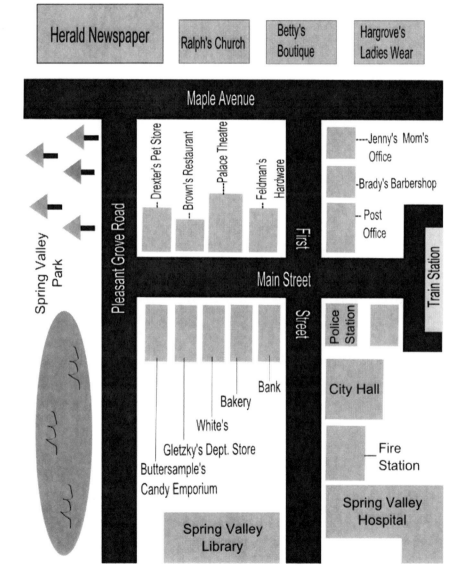

CHAPTER 1

"WE'RE NEARING OUR DESTINATION," ANNOUNCED the first officer to his captain. "Planet Earth is straight ahead."

"I am approaching the space pod," reported the captain as he stepped off his elevator and entered the area of the ship where the pod was located. Inside the pod, the captain sat down in one of only two seats that were available in the vessel. "I am starting ignition sequence," he pronounced while strapping himself in. Then he pushed a series of buttons and the space pod's engines ignited, thrusting powerfully away.

The space pod dashed off towards Earth, making sure its presence wasn't detected by the planet's surveillance systems. The egg-shaped pod spun its way down to the earth's surface, broke through the clouds and headed for the town of Spring Valley. Rapidly, it spun its way to the Valleydale subdivision. It maneuvered its way over Springhaven Court and the home of one Ralph Eltison.

As it landed, steam emitted from the bottom of the pod and filled the air that surrounded the Eltison backyard. Underneath their willow tree and next to the doghouse, stood Ralph Eltison and his ever-faithful superhero dog, Elt. They waited patiently for the Trianthian leader to make his appearance.

The door to the pod opened. From the darkness inside the pod emerged the familiar glowing figure of Coladeus. He hopped down from the pod and walked over to both Ralph and Elt. He first shook Ralph's hand, and then Elt's right paw.

"So good to see you both, my friends from Earth," remarked Coladeus.

Ralph's excitement was all too noticeable. "What assignment do you have for us Coladeus? Are we going to travel back with you and save a solar system or discover a lost planet?"

"Why all that and more," assured Coladeus as he welcomed the boy and his dog into his pod. "Usually there is only room for two occupants in our pod, but we have made special arrangements in order to accommodate you both on board Trianthius I."

"That's cool!" exalted Ralph. "When can we leave?"

"Well...right now," answered Coladeus.

The three boarded the ship and fastened their restraints. In an instant, the space pod blasted off for Trianthius I, which was safely orbiting Earth.

"Can we help steer?" asked Ralph.

"Why sure," smiled Coladeus. Elt's tail wagged slowly as he watched his human take control of the Trianthian space pod. Ralph was excited yet careful in his efforts to steer the pod in the right direction.

"We should see Trianthius I shortly," stated Coladeus.

"There it is!" yelled Ralph. "I'll get us close to the ship." Coladeus watched Ralph carefully as he guided the space pod under the belly of the Trianthian ship.

"She's beautiful!" exclaimed Ralph. Ralph's eyes lit up brighter than ever as he took in all the wonderful sights before him. The greenish, triangular-shaped vessel welcomed the smaller vessel as the pod attached itself to Trianthius I. Coladeus glanced over at both Ralph and Elt.

"Ralph, lunch time!" exclaimed Coladeus. "I fixed some sandwiches."

Ralph stared at the Trianthian elder for a few seconds, and then realized where he really was. He had never left his backyard. Ralph was sitting on top of Elt's doghouse, straddling the roof. Elt had slunk inside the doghouse, taking a rest from the summer's heat and humidity. Ralph's dad stuck his head out the door. He held a plate full of sandwiches. "Well, are you coming?"

"Coming Dad!" shouted Ralph as he leaped off the doghouse and ran up the porch and into the kitchen. Elt followed him but opted to enter through the doggie door.

It had been a couple of weeks since Ralph had last seen the REAL Trianthian leader late one summer night in his backyard. It was the night Coladeus had revealed both his identity and purpose for visiting Elt. Ever since then, Ralph could only wonder about the nature of Elt's next mission. Was he, ten year-old Ralph Eltison, going to be part of that mission?

Although Ralph had cut the daydreaming down quite a bit, knowing his dog, still technically a pup, was a hero with super powers, was just too exciting. Adventures of traveling through space filled Ralph's head. He knew that at any moment, a voice from Elt's collar would communicate with them. He thought about voyages to unknown worlds, or space adventures to distant planets. It was overwhelming!

Ralph wanted to tell someone, but he knew he couldn't. Not to just anyone. He wanted to share that secret with his best friend, Jenny Rodgers. Jenny wouldn't tell anyone, he knew that. But informing one more human was that much more critical to Elt's existence as a super dog.

It had only been a couple of weeks since Elt and his friends, the pets from the Valleydale subdivision, had thwarted a bank robbery and captured Frake and most of the other men working for the unscrupulous Walter E. Crum. The town of Spring Valley was still abuzz. Folks were out shopping, working, and playing. There were no more worries. Frake and his men were in jail and Crum had flown off in his helicopter, hopefully never to be seen again. The park was full of people and their pets. Life was great again in Spring Valley.

The month of July was nearing its long, hot end. Ralph, his dad, and Elt had just returned from a mini-vacation, an almost week-long camping trip in the mountains that overlooked Spring Valley. Elt got to experience firsthand what outdoor living was all about; those late night trips to battle Crum and his men did not count as outdoor living.

They slept in a tent, fished for some of their food, burned a campfire each night, and hiked miles and miles each day. There was a lake for fishing, swimming, and sightseeing. Now, nothing beat sleeping at the foot of Ralph's bed every night, but outdoor living wasn't so bad. Elt was doubly happy, for Ralph's dad had administered the proper flea and tick treatments before they left. Scratching and biting for five days would have been no fun at all.

When Ralph, his dad, and Elt returned home, normalcy resumed. Ralph's dad went back to work. Ralph completed his chores in the mornings. Some of the chores included bathing Elt, dumping the garbage, and washing the dishes. These chores were different from the ones he and his dad accomplished together, like yard work and cleaning house.

Ralph worked on his daily chores in the morning so he could free up his afternoon time for Jenny, Bernadette, and Elt. After Jenny returned home from her grandparent's house, Ralph and Elt would walk over. For close to an hour before dinner time, they would stroll along their usual route; Valleydale Drive to Schoolhouse Road and back, then all the way over to Springhaven Court, where Ralph and Elt lived.

The kids and their dogs would pass by all the neighborhood pets. Juan, the Chihuahua was always ready to greet them as they strolled by. Sarge would venture out from his doghouse, catch a glimpse of the kids and their dogs, belt out a couple of warning barks, and then head right back into his doghouse or scratch at the door for Mr. Davis to let him in. Max stayed inside with Mrs. Petrie, for it was still very hot outside and the old boy loved the air conditioning. Chin remained in the back of his house, only peeking to be sure that it was Elt and Bernadette, and then withdrawing to the shelter of his doghouse.

Jasmine, the tabby cat would sometimes trek along with the kids and pets, but would generally head back to her house when they reached Schoolhouse Road. Although she could handle the on-coming traffic from automobiles on that road, she figured that by then she had spent enough time tagging along with the walkers.

The last pet in their neighborhood was Prince, the highly decorated Doberman Pinscher. Ralph and Elt would catch a glimpse of Prince and Mr. Dawkins strolling in their yard. Prince would give a nod to both Elt and Bernadette. His demeanor was very stoic, nothing like the friendlier version of himself that helped Elt and the Valleydale pets thwart the criminal intentions of Walter E. Crum and his men.

Elt and the other neighborhood pets hadn't held a meeting since the heroic feats of a few weeks ago. A meeting was in the works, but Sarge hadn't announced it yet and Jasmine hadn't delivered the message to anyone. Elt had been on vacation with his humans. The Davis's and Mrs. Petrie had just returned from their vacations. Anyway, there was no real news to report amongst the pets in the neighborhood. Everything was calm. Late summer was in fact pretty non-eventful. Things, however, were about to change.

The day after returning from camping, Ralph finished lunch and asked his dad if he could head over to Jenny's house with Elt. Mr. Eltison and Ralph had finished their chores earlier, so Ralph was soon out the door with Elt, his leash in hand. When Elt and Ralph passed Mrs. Petrie's house on the corner of Springhaven Court and Valleydale Drive, they stopped to gaze at the house in between Jenny's and Mrs. Petrie's.

A sizeable yellow and green moving truck was parked in the driveway. Two men clad in khaki one-piece jumpsuits were transporting furniture and boxes into the house. Someone was moving in, but who? There were no signs of anyone other than the two men from the moving company.

When Ralph and Elt arrived at Jenny's house, Jenny was seated on her side porch with Bernadette lying near her feet. Jenny too had been watching the events next door.

"Have you seen who's moving in?" asked Ralph.

"Not yet," replied Jenny. "But I did see the moving guys take a couple of bikes to the garage."

"Kid's bikes?" asked Ralph.

"Yep," returned Jenny.

The yellow ranch house had only been vacant for about two weeks. An older couple, the Pattersons, had lived in the house for about ten years. Their children had grown and moved out of state, so they decided to find a smaller home that was closer to their kids and grandchildren. The couple's house had almost met the fate of the devious Walter Crum, for Frake was purchasing any home he could in order to charge renters very high rates. Now Crum was nowhere to be found and most of his men were behind bars. A "FOR SALE" sign had appeared as soon as the couple left and now someone new was moving in.

Jenny and Ralph watched for a few minutes, but no one other than the movers stepped in and out of the yellow ranch house. They knew that sooner or later they would meet the new people, so Ralph, Jenny, and their pooches proceeded with their walk. Upon their return however, Ralph and Jenny eagerly sat down on the side porch to continue watching the yellow house, while Elt and Bernadette found a shady area below them in the grass.

The moving truck was gone. Other than an old green car in the driveway, there was still no sign of anyone actually moving in and out of the house. Finally, something happened. The front door opened and a middle-aged man appeared. He was tall, a couple of inches over six feet, and he had brown hair with a fair complexion. As he headed towards the car, he noticed the kids and their pets.

"Well hello!" greeted the man. His accent was different; he was definitely not from Spring Valley or any of its surrounding counties. The kids were caught off guard by the man's friendly greeting. "What lovely puppies," the man continued. He proceeded to the fence and laid his long, lanky hands on top of it. Jenny regained herself enough to reply.

"Thank you," she answered brightly. Jenny jumped off the porch and walked over to the fence, tugging lightly on Bernadette's leash. The Cocker Spaniel rose from her resting spot and followed her human. Ralph and Elt moved forward too. The man reached over to pet the two dogs.

"You must have a wonderful time with these stunning puppies," said the man. Both Elt and Bernadette sniffed the man's hands, and then generously licked them. They sensed that he was a good human, not suspicious like Crum or Frake.

"You're not from around here Mister," mentioned Ralph. "You sound like you're from England."

"Oh, pardon my manners," returned the man. "I'm Stanley Greenlee…Professor Stanley Greenlee to be correct. And yes, I am from Great Britain." He held out his right hand as a friendly gesture.

Jenny forged ahead of Ralph to shake the professor's hand. "My name is Jenny Rodgers," she said. "And this is Ralph...Ralph Eltison."

"And these are our dogs," interjected Ralph. "Elt and Bernadette." Professor Greenlee bent over once again to pet the pups.

"Uh Mister, I mean Professor?" asked Ralph. "Do you have any pets?"

"Why yes we do," answered the professor. "A dog and a cat to be exact, along with two very special individuals. Ah, here comes one of them now."

Out from the front door, running down the steps, was a boy. He too had brown hair and a fair complexion, but was freckled. He looked to be about the same age as Ralph and Jenny.

"Come along son," said the professor. "Come meet your new neighbors."

"Technically, I live down the street," said Ralph. "Jenny lives here, but I guess I'm still a neighbor." Jenny smiled at the boy, who ran over and stood beside his dad.

"Precisely," returned the professor. He glanced down at his son. "See I told you there would be other children here." The boy smiled. Professor Greenlee turned around and headed over to his car.

"Cheerio!" exclaimed the boy to Ralph and Jenny. "Me name is Bryan...Bryan Greenlee."

Cheerio? What was that? Cereal? Ralph displayed a puzzled expression, glanced at Jenny with that same expression, and then turned back to greet Bryan awkwardly. "Uh...greetings."

Jenny knew exactly what the boy from Great Britain was saying. That brand of cereal was actually named for the British greeting. She returned a smile and said "Hi."

Jenny and Ralph were still standing near the fence with Elt and Bernadette. Bryan knelt down to gaze at the pups through the fence holes. He slipped his fingers through to touch each dog. "We picked up our puppy last year while on holiday in France," mentioned Bryan as he continued to pet Elt and Bernadette.

"Which holiday? Christmas?" asked Ralph. Bryan displayed a puzzled look. Jenny shook her head and smiled.

"What he's trying to say," explained Jenny, "is that his family bought a dog while on vacation in France."

"There ya go," said a smiling Bryan.

"My name is Jenny, this is Ralph," returned Jenny. "And our dogs are Elt and Bernadette." Bryan glanced at the dogs briefly and then turned his head around, as if he were searching for someone.

"Let me see if I can fetch me sister," said Bryan. He placed two of his fingers from his left hand to his mouth and belted out a shriek of a whistle. It only took a few seconds before a young girl in a light blue dress scurried out from the backyard. She was about two-thirds as tall as Bryan; with brown hair, freckles, and the same fair complexion as her dad and brother. Behind her, a black toy poodle and a black and white cat followed, but they stopped and hid behind the girl's legs. Both Elt and Bernadette had noticed the dog and cat. Their ears had perked up and they both stood at attention. They wanted to meet the neighborhood's newest pets.

"This is me little sister Caroline," announced Bryan. "She is eight years old."

"Pleased to meet your acquaintance," said Caroline as she curtsied to both Ralph and Jenny.

"This is Ralph and Jenny, our new neighbors," said Bryan to his sister. "They look to be about ten, like me."

Jenny smiled. "We are ten."

Caroline bent down to pet her poodle. "This is Trixie. She is almost two years old. Daddy purchased her in France."

"She's beautiful," said Jenny.

"And this is Seymour, our kitty cat," continued Caroline. Seymour rubbed his face against the girl's legs. All eyes, though, were still focused on the toy poodle, Trixie. She bashfully lowered her head. Trixie was used to gazes and stares, for she truly was a beauty to behold. She was jet black in color and finely groomed, for there wasn't one strand of fur out of place. She was gracefully trimmed with pink bows on both her head and tail; her nails even seemed polished. Trixie's petite figure was cleanly shaven; it was as if she went to the poodle groomer daily. Her eyes…well let's just say that those brown beauties, along with her dazzling, long eyelashes, could melt many a male canine's heart.

Trixie raised her head and slowly stepped in front of Caroline. She couldn't help noticing the two canines in front of her, especially the handsome black and brown Labrador-Collie mix. She gleamed at Bernadette, but quickly diverted all attention towards Elt.

Now Elt only knew one female pooch and that was Bernadette. They were pals, and they really cared for each other. Their relationship, though, was similar to that of their humans. Ralph and Jenny were best friends, and that was it.

Still, there emerged a certain territorial jealousy factor on behalf of Bernadette. She had never had to compete with any other female for attention. She wasn't amused when Trixie flashed "the look" at Elt. If there was a "stink eye" given by dogs to each other, then Bernadette was really giving it to Trixie. The poodle, however, paid no attention to her female counterpart. Her eyes were totally fixed on Elt.

Elt couldn't help it. He didn't know why, but he couldn't keep his eyes off of the beautiful Trixie. He had never seen such a stunning creature. Bernadette watched the two pooches gaze at each other as long as she could stand it. Then she stepped ahead and moved in front of Elt, keeping her reddish-brown tail high in the air, blocking their view of each other.

"You're going to like our school," noted Jenny.

"And the park and pool," added Ralph. Professor Greenlee smiled and placed one of his pale, lanky hands on each of his children's shoulders. Both Bryan and Caroline smiled as they peered up at their dad.

"I'm sure they're going to have a jolly good time here," said the professor. "Now I've got quite a bit of work to finish here kids. Don't forget to help your Mum with the boxes in the garage. Jenny...Ralph, we'll have to have you up at the campus one day after I've got settled in. Cheerio!"

"Bye," said Ralph and Jenny simultaneously. Professor Greenlee turned around, walked over to his car, and grabbed a box from inside. Then he walked into his house through the front door.

"Is your dad like a scientist or something?" asked Ralph. Both Caroline and Bryan nodded yes.

"What does he study?" asked Jenny. "The moon? The stars?"

"Don't really know," answered Bryan. "Scientists have to maintain secrecy when they're working on something top secret."

"That's so cool!" gushed Ralph. "I kind of know what my dad does, but not really."

"I know my mom works in an office and talks to people on the phone," added Jenny. "I wish she was a scientist."

"Are you going to help your dad with any experiments?" asked Ralph.

"Don't know yet," answered Bryan. "Maybe."

"We better go help Mother," reminded Caroline. Bryan nodded his head.

"See ya around," yelled Bryan as he and Caroline ran back to their house. Trixie and Seymour followed. Trixie took one last glance at Elt, and then coyly turned away, as if she were sad to leave.

Jenny and Ralph sat back down on the side porch. Bernadette followed, but Elt remained frozen in place, mesmerized by Trixie even after she had gone. Bernadette couldn't believe it. Never in her short life had she ever witnessed Elt like this. Who was that poodle and what had she done to Elt? Bernadette yelped out a series of short barks. The fourth bark finally snapped Elt out of his trance. He glanced around. Trixie and Seymour had disappeared inside the house. Bernadette glared at Elt. It seemed that there was a little jealousy going on, but the story on the two dogs was that they were friends, like their humans Ralph and Jenny. Elt turned around and joined Bernadette by the porch.

Jenny's mom then opened the door and handed the two kids a glass of lemonade each. She also brought a bowl full of cold water for Elt and Bernadette. The two pooches stood up and started quenching their thirst with the fresh, cool water.

After the lemonade, it was about time for Ralph and Elt to return home. Bernadette followed Jenny as she headed in the door. Ralph watched the Cocker Spaniel. "Hey Jenny?" he asked.

"What's up?" asked Jenny.

"Never thought about it much until now," said Ralph. "Why did you name her Bernadette?"

Jenny smiled. "That's easy," she answered. "That's my mom's favorite song. See ya tomorrow." Jenny and Bernadette went inside. Ralph nodded, turned around and reached for Elt's leash. The two headed back to their house.

Ralph couldn't wait to tell his dad the exciting news about the new neighbors! Although there were quite a few pets in Ralph and

Jenny's neighborhood, there weren't many kids. Ralph and Jenny would sometimes play with kids in adjoining neighborhoods, but in their immediate area, Ralph and Jenny were the only children. Now two kids had just moved in, and their ages were very close to that of Ralph's and Jenny's. Plus, they had two pets! Would Bryan and Caroline enjoy walking Trixie and possibly Seymour with Ralph and Jenny's pets?

The Greenlees' arrival had certainly caught the attention of Ralph, Jenny, Elt, and Bernadette, but another figure also noticed the new family. Perched quietly on the fence between Mrs. Petrie's yard and the Greenlee's yard was Jasmine the tabby cat, who had witnessed the whole scene. Elt may have been interested in Trixie the toy poodle; Jasmine's attention, however, was drawn to Seymour the cat. She watched Seymour's every move before he disappeared into the Greenlees' house.

Jasmine had been the only cat in the immediate neighborhood. Was she going to enjoy having another cat to hang out with? Jasmine leaped down and dashed across the street toward Sarge's house. Surely a neighborhood meeting was in order to discuss the arrival of Trixie and Seymour.

CHAPTER 2

"JUBILANT" AND "ECSTATIC" WERE TWO words that best described the overall feelings of Spring Valley's citizens and pets. Thanks to the heroic efforts of Elt and his friends from the Valleydale subdivision, the black cloud that had hung over the town had been lifted. There were no more worries or fears.

The downtown streets were full of busy shoppers and walkers. Main Street had never been so vibrant. Folks were elated that they could go shopping, eat at a restaurant, or catch a flick without fear of something unfortunate happening to them. The aromas of freshly popped popcorn and heavenly baked bread permeated the air on Main Street. Feldman's and Gletzky's stores were filled with eager shoppers. Brown's Restaurant boasted long lines of hungry patrons. The soda fountain at White's was booming with customers, too. The town had been restored.

The town's business leaders were very grateful. They appreciated the daring efforts set forth by Elt and his friends in capturing Frake and his men. To show their gratitude, many of the town's business leaders offered the Valleydale pet owners free gifts and services. For instance,

Mr. Brady offered Ralph and his dad free haircuts at his barber shop. Ralph's dad kindly accepted a free haircut for Ralph, only once, though Mr. Brady insisted that Ralph's haircuts were "on him" any time.

The pet owners were given free meals at Brown's, free movie passes at the Palace Theatre, and free loaves of fresh bread at the bakery. Even though the pet owners were indeed citizens themselves of Spring Valley, they enjoyed a certain "celebrity status," as their pets were indeed famous. But they took their celebrity in stride, for they knew that the citizens of Spring Valley were thankful, and simply wanted to show their appreciation in any way possible.

Now Spring Valley wasn't the only town that truly celebrated Crum's demise. The citizens of Bordertown were even more elated to hear the news about the misfortunes of Walter Eugene Crum and his cronies. The dome of unhappiness and fear was slowly lifted. Folks in the town were smiling, laughing, and joking. Factories still billowed smoke and the streets were still unsightly, but the air of happiness helped move the overall demeanor of Bordertown in the right direction.

The day of the failed robbery attempt at the Spring Valley National Bank was also the last time Crum had been seen. Crum, Sid and the pilot had dashed off in the old man's helicopter over downtown Spring Valley. There were a few Crum "sightings" around town, although none were confirmed. Folks who snooped around outside Crum's mansion thought they saw a head move in and out of the upstairs windows. It might have been the old man, but it also could have been the maid or the butler, as the two had decided to stay on at Crum's estate and await their boss's return.

The residents weren't the only ones searching for Crum. Even police officers from Bordertown were searching for him. Now that he had been linked to the bank robberies in Spring Valley, Walter Crum, the wealthy businessman, was a fugitive. Although Crum's factories and businesses were still operating during his absence, Walter Crum's fortune and influence had been greatly diminished. Citizens in Bordertown weren't paying Frake and his boys for protection anymore. Many of Crum's properties had been taken by the local authorities and sold to new owners.

Citizens who were too scared to challenge Crum earlier, now began to revitalize Bordertown. The mayor decreed that a city park be erected, containing a swimming pool and other recreational venues, so that both adults and kids could have fun again. Many townspeople who couldn't start their own businesses before, now opened shops like a toy and video store, along with a bowling alley. Bordertown was becoming a decent place to live.

Still, there were some folks in Bordertown that didn't feel the town would ever be safe from the clutches of Crum and his men. They decided to move their families elsewhere. Many of them decided to move to Spring Valley, since peace had been restored to the idyllic town. One such fellow was named Henry Quincy Buttersample.

Henry Q. Buttersample was born in Bordertown, a brother to three younger siblings. They lived in an old, deteriorated slum house that Henry's mother and father rented from Crum. Henry's mother and father both worked in one of Crum's factories, barely earning enough money to pay the rent, electricity, water, or to feed a family of six. Many times Henry would give his dinner to one of his younger family members. Henry helped his parents out greatly by completing his chores and watching his younger siblings until his parents returned home from work.

Henry didn't earn any money for his chores, but instead his dad would reward him with one treat. Every Friday, his father would come home, lay his belongings on his desk, reach into his pocket, and hand Henry his reward…a small piece of candy. Sometimes it was a piece of chocolate. Other times it was butterscotch, a hot cinnamon flavored jawbreaker, or even a piece of bubble gum. His father never forgot. Even when Henry was older, and raised a family of his own, Henry's dad would surprise him sometimes with a small piece of candy.

Henry finished high school, but had no money for college. His parents became ill for a while, so Henry's only choice was to work at the local clothing factory and support his family. He worked seven days a week, earning just enough money to feed them all. Although Henry worked in a factory that produced clothing and shoes, he had a dream of running his own business involving his passion…candy. Henry Q. Buttersample longed to open both a factory that manufactured candy, and a store that sold it for kids and adults.

As Henry grew older, he met the love of his life, Emma. Henry and Emma married and had four children. After being promoted to a supervisor's position at the clothing factory, Henry bought a house, and his folks moved in with his family. His brother and sisters also lived in Bordertown, and had families of their own. Henry still dreamed of his candy business.

Opening a candy store in Walter Crum's Bordertown wasn't a grand idea at all. First, if Crum didn't have anything to do with it, it wasn't going to happen at all. Second, candy was a fun thing; something that made folks, young and old, happy. Bordertown wasn't a happy place. So the day that the news spread about Walter Crum's demise, Henry knew that the time had come to fulfill his dream. But there was still that nagging doubt about Crum's return to Bordertown, so Henry had to make a tough decision. Henry and his family moved to Spring Valley.

Providentially, Henry chose the one site in Spring Valley that was a perfect location for a candy store. Although it had been the hideout of Frake and his men, the former W.E.C. Insurance building, (and before that, Jessup's) had a bottom floor which had been vacant for a couple of months. On one hot summer day in July, Henry Q. Buttersample visited the site with his wife and started his dream. To their surprise, they discovered that the second floor apartment was vacant, too. The folks who had previously rented from Frake had moved out and found a cheaper location. The Spring Valley National Bank had taken over the rent and sale of the building, so Mrs. Samuels from the bank and the Buttersamples sealed the deal a few days later.

Even though he had lived a very meager life, Henry had managed to set a few dollars aside through the years. He could now use the money he had saved to initiate the project. The Buttersamples sold their house in Bordertown and moved into the second floor apartment, grandparents and all.

With the assistance of a loan from the Spring Valley National Bank, Henry was able to buy all the appliances, furniture, and building materials necessary to create the candy emporium he had dreamed about for so many years. With his savings, Henry purchased taffy and licorice machines. He also acquired a couple of ovens that would help create his chocolate candies and fudge. Then there was the cotton candy machine, a ribbon candy contraption, and a chocolate fountain. He ordered plentiful amounts of cocoa, sugar, milk, coconut, mixed nuts, marshmallows, and other confectionary supplies. He made sure his candy store had enough display cases to hold all the tasty treasures he was going to offer.

The candy production was truly a family business. Emma quickly learned how to operate all of the candy-making equipment. The kids served, cooked, and cleaned. Henry's mom and dad, although elderly, insisted on helping too. One would run the cash register while the other would greet customers, all to help the business succeed.

Henry cooked his own chocolate, including the various flavors of fudge: chocolate, vanilla and peanut butter to name just a few. He created his own licorice, toffee, and taffy. His store sold multi-flavored gum, hard candy, gummies of many shapes and sizes, button candy, red hot cinnamon candies, and powdered candy. Henry showcased hundreds of tantalizing chocolates that included truffles, turtles, caramels, and chocolate covered cherries. In one short month, the former W.E.C. Insurance Company had been transformed into BUTTERSAMPLE'S CANDY EMPORIUM. Hundreds of eager children, along with their parents, awaited the opening of Spring Valley's first real candy store ever!

Now in Spring Valley's history, the downtown had showcased a wide variety of retail businesses. There had been a few general stores and department stores, like Gletzky's, that offered candy, including chocolates. There was, though, never really an authentic candy "factory" that produced many of their sweet delicacies right there in their own store.

News spread fast about the candy store's opening day which would be at ten in the morning on a Saturday in late July. The Herald newspaper triumphed a dynamic one page ad a week before the big day. There were ads on the radio and television. There were even dozens of advertisements on the internet.

Back in the Valleydale subdivision, Ralph heard the news from Jenny, who had seen the humongous ad in the newspaper. The best part was that the first one hundred kids who entered Buttersample's on opening day would receive a free piece of candy of their choice.

"Can we go Saturday?" Ralph asked his dad.

"I don't see why not," replied Mr. Eltison.

"Can I take Elt?"

"Ralph, unfortunately, dogs aren't allowed in places that sell any type of food, including candy," said Mr. Eltison.

"Yeah, I know," answered Ralph hopefully. "But Mr. Drexel does in his store. We'll be right across the street."

"So a field trip, huh?" asked Mr. Eltison.

"Can we?"

Ralph's dad smiled. "I see you've thought this one out for a while."

Ralph smiled. "I'll call Jenny."

After a few minutes of persuasion, Jenny's mom agreed. So the plan was set. The kids would bring Elt and Bernadette. Their parents would watch the dogs while they toured the candy emporium, and then they would escort their pooches to Drexel's and purchase some delicious treats for them.

Ralph and Jenny weren't the only ones who knew about the candy store. Bryan and Caroline, the "new kids on the block," saw the commercial on television. When Professor Greenlee returned home from work, he was confronted by two very eager, friendly candy lovers. They both screamed and jumped into their father's arms when he approved. "Okay, okay," said a chuckling Professor Greenlee as the kids continued to hug their dad.

When Saturday morning arrived, Ralph and Jenny were up at the crack of dawn. In fact, Ralph hadn't been so excited since the day after Coladeus had visited Elt in his backyard. It was seven o'clock, and the plan by both families was to arrive by eight. Surely, arriving two hours ahead of the scheduled opening would be early enough to ensure the kids received the free candy. Plus, there was always the bragging rights thing that kids claimed whenever they got to do something before anyone else. It was sometimes an adult thing, too.

After a helping of dry dog food, Elt ventured outside, took care of business, and then retrieved the morning paper for Ralph's dad. Ralph downed a quick bowl of cereal, then dressed and waited outside his dad's room.

Elt had no idea what was going on. He saw his human pick up the leash. It was too early for a walk. Was he going to the vet's office? Was it another camping trip? There were no tents or luggage. All

Ralph grabbed was the leash, and soon Elt was in the truck with his humans.

The Eltisons stopped at Jenny's house. Ms. Rodgers, Jenny, and Bernadette were just stepping out, ready to leave. "We'll follow you," said Ms. Rodgers as she opened her car door. Just then, the neighbors' front door opened, and out ran the Greenlee children.

"Where ya going?" asked Bryan.

Jenny rolled down her window. "To Buttersample's," she said.

"We are too," said Caroline. "But dogs aren't allowed."

"No," replied Jenny. "My mom is going to watch Bernadette while I go in, and then we're taking Bernadette to Drexel's."

"What's Drexels?" asked Bryan.

"The pet store. It's right across the street from the candy factory." When Professor and Mrs. Greenlee appeared, they were met by two even more excited kids with one question.

"Mom, Dad, please can we take Trixie and Seymour to the pet store after we visit the candy emporium?" asked both Bryan and Caroline simultaneously. The Greenlees appeared slightly confused for a few seconds, but then recognized the two cars filled with neighbors and their pets. After gathering information from Mrs. Rodgers, the Greenlees understood what was happening. Professor Greenlee stepped back inside the house, whistled, and then exited with two leashes. Trixie and Seymour followed.

Trixie's appearance once again caught Elt's attention, and Berandette's too, for different reasons. As Trixie and Seymour followed their humans into the car, Elt paid close attention to the poodle. "Wow, Elt really notices the new dog," observed Mr. Eltison.

"He acted the same way the day Jenny and I met them," returned Ralph.

When the caravan of three vehicles passed by Buttersample's moments later, the kids were relieved to see that there were only a handful of children and parents waiting outside. The parents parked their cars in a lot behind Buttersample's and joined the small line that had formed. It was close to eight o'clock.

By nine o'clock, the crowd started to increase steadily. In fact, by nine forty-five, almost two hundred men, women, and children formed a line that stretched all the way down Main and First Streets, all the way past the Spring Valley National Bank.

Now, while the kids were patiently waiting for the doors to open, there was drama going on in "pet world." Just as he had felt when he first met her, Elt was totally mesmerized by Trixie. He watched every move she made. He tugged slightly on his leash, but had to remember not to show too much strength, no matter how badly he wanted to sit beside her.

Bernadette, however, didn't want anything to do with that situation. She sat patiently by her Jenny, but still gazed over at Elt once in a while. She couldn't believe it. Elt was going crazy over Trixie. Seymour remained stoic beside the poodle, while Trixie knew that she was the center of attention.

Everyone's attention suddenly turned forward when the front door opened and out strode Henry Q. Buttersample. He was clad in a black tuxedo, white shirt, black shoes, and a red bowtie. His tidy hair was parted to the side. Once outside, Henry just stopped and gazed at the crowd before him. Never in a million years did he expect such a gathering. He took a few steps forward, turned around, and then faced the crowd again. From the corner of his eye, Henry noticed the kids and parents with their pets almost near the front of the line.

"Good morning boys and girls…ladies and gentlemen…canines and felines!" shouted Henry Buttersample. "Welcome to Buttersample's Candy Emporium, Spring Valley's one and only Candy Wonderland!" The crowd began to clap and cheer loudly. Humbled, Henry bowed. He then straightened his bowtie. "Now, before we enter this amazing establishment," he began, "I want to make an announcement. I know I promised the first one-hundred children a free piece of candy, but I'm afraid I can't afford to stay at that number." Henry paused, his face solemn. There was a collective "aw" in the audience. "Instead, I've decided to UP that number to the first two hundred!" Buttersample threw out his hands and grinned broadly. There were roars from the crowd, especially when the back half of the crowd heard the news. Now pretty much everyone in line was going to receive a free piece of candy.

"Now I also want to say that I have a special treat in store for the first twenty children who woke up really early today and were the first ones in line," continued the candy man. Jenny, Ralph, Bryan, and Caroline all gasped at each other, grinned, and then focused right back on Buttersample. "To the first twenty children, I'll give a personal tour of the candy factory, where all the wonder and magic takes place!"

There were many "oohs" and "ahs" emanating from the crowd, for the first twenty children were about to receive the most exciting and awesome tour of their lives. Ralph and Jenny smiled and gave each other "fist bumps." Bryan and Caroline jumped up and down.

"Are you ready, children?" shouted Henry.

"Yes!" answered the boisterous crowd.

"Then Mr. Mayor, let's cut the ribbon and let the children in!" Mayor Helms trotted up to the front doors. He had been mingling with the crowd up and down the line on Main Street. He carried with him an over-sized pair of scissors, which he held up high for everyone to witness. The crowd cheered him on.

"It is my honor, as the Mayor of the greatest town in the world," heralded Mayor Helms, "to hereby officially open Buttersample's Candy Emporium!" The throng continued to cheer while the mayor surrounded the ribbon with his over-sized pair of scissors and cut the ribbon with a flourish. The kids in front of the line inched closer to the entrance. Then Mayor Helms and Henry Buttersample threw open the front doors simultaneously. Everyone who could see, leaned, stretched, and jumped just to get a peek of what was inside.

Henry approached the front of the line and began to count, letting the first twenty children proceed. As Jenny and Ralph passed by him, Henry noticed Ms. Rodgers and Mr. Eltison holding the pets' leashes. He then noticed that there was another set of parents with pets on leashes.

"I'm sorry, but pets aren't allowed in our establishment," said Henry softly.

"That's okay," assured Jenny. "They're here for Drexel's after we're finished." Henry smiled and nodded in understanding, then bent down to pet Elt and Bernadette.

"What wonderful dogs," commented Henry.

"Thanks," said Ralph. "My name is Ralph, and she's Jenny. My dog's name is Elt, and that's Bernadette."

Henry rubbed his chin while he petted the two dogs in front of him. "Their names sound familiar."

Both Elt and Bernadette sensed the goodness in Henry, and welcomed his gesture; not like the feeling they encountered when they met Frake and his brother at the park during the Memorial Day Weekend Celebration.

"You may have heard about them in the newspaper recently," said Mr. Eltison. "These pups are heroes."

"That's it!" exalted Henry. "These are the fantastic animals that stopped the bank robbery!"

"What bank robbery?" interjected Professor Greenlee.

"We'll fill you in," said Ms. Rodgers. Ralph and Jenny waved bye to their parents and entered the candy factory. Bryan and Caroline walked up to Buttersample.

"Are these two more heroes?" questioned Henry.

"Heroes?" asked Bryan.

"No sir, we just moved to Spring Valley," answered Professor Greenlee.

Henry bent down to touch Trixie and Seymour this time. "That's splendid. I bet they're heroes to your family." Bryan and Caroline smiled, then moved ahead to the entrance, followed by the rest of the lucky group of twenty.

"We'll be here waiting for you," called Mrs. Greenlee.

"Have a jolly good time," added the professor.

Henry rose and finished his count. "I'll be back in a jiffy!" announced he, and then the doors closed. Once inside, the kids couldn't believe the unbelievable, magical scene that stood before them. No one could have ever imagined that the space that was once used by Frake and his men would be transformed into a candy wonderland. It was truly an amazing achievement.

Instead of several rooms, the entire first floor was one mammoth arena, only divided by the candy counter that split the factory from the candy store. The walls, ceilings, and floors were enhanced with bright reds, oranges, and yellows. There were several neatly designed shelves, each filled with boxes of assorted chocolates, candies, fudges, and cookies.

The aroma inside was sweet heaven. It was difficult to pinpoint the exact scent, being more like an array of sweet, warm, and tantalizing aromas all designed to melt hearts and stomachs.

Henry described to the children in great detail all of the delicacies that surrounded the lobby area; chocolates from his own candy factory and some ordered from all corners of the globe. Henry then turned to face the main candy counter that divided the lobby from the factory. It was enormous!

There were hundreds of different chocolates, laid in perfect rows, displayed in the candy cases. Chocolate caramels, cream filled chocolates, and even delights filled with strawberries and cherries. There were lollipops, licorice, cinnamon sticks, and button candy. To the right of the cash register were three delightful chocolate fountains; one dark, one white, and one regular, all flowing with rich, smooth, liquid chocolate. There was a sampling tray of strawberries, bananas, and sweet bread situated right next to the fountains for the customers to taste as they shopped for all the goodies.

It was a challenge for Henry Buttersample to keep twenty young minds focused on the tour. Once he guided them away from the candy displays, they were able to adjust their attention to something new and exciting. "This is where all the magic happens," announced Henry.

The group had entered the confectionary factory. Henry's first stop was the taffy machine. His son William was creating the delicious, multi-colored taffy. William scooped a pile of wrapped taffy into a decorative box, then sealed the box and placed it on a table behind him.

William's sister Elaine monitored the cotton candy and licorice machines, with the assistance of an associate of the store. The kids whispered to each other and pointed to the sights that excited them most. Henry explained the features of each device only briefly, for he let the scenery before the crowd do all the talking.

The fudge and chocolate ovens followed. Mrs. Buttersample supervised her associates while her two younger children played in a small area away from all of the hot equipment. There were dozens of flat trays lined perfectly with chocolates and fudges awaiting their final destination- the candy case display.

Bryan and Caroline stared at the wonders all around them. On their holidays in Europe, they had witnessed some pretty spectacular events, but this visit to the candy emporium seemed to blow all other things away. Ralph and Jenny stayed right with their new friends. They too were in awe of the sweetness that surrounded them.

As the tour ended, it was time for the free sample. As the children headed back to the candy displays, they were met by Henry's parents, who showcased a tantalizing array of chocolates, hard candies, and gummies for the children to choose from. Ralph chose a cordial cherry while Jenny selected a truffle. Caroline and Bryan each chose miniature lollipops; one green and one red. After the sampling, the children were given ten minutes to shop and make their choices, before the next group could enter, retrieve their free samples, and then shop to their hearts' content.

It was a very profitable day for Henry Buttersample and his family. The candy store and factory earned more money in one day than Henry had earned in one month at the clothing factory. The folks of Spring Valley, elated that there was this new, exciting place to visit and shop in, rewarded Henry and his family quite generously.

As the doors opened and the first group of kids exited the candy store with fancy, clear bags of assorted candies gripped tightly, the dogs plus one cat perked up to see their humans once again. Elt wondered why he couldn't enter the candy store with his human. Little did he know that a trip to his "candy store" was next on the "to do" list for that day. Mr. Drexel always passed out free treats to the pets that visited his store. There would also be an additional goodie bag going home with Elt and his humans.

Bernadette's tail started to wag when she saw Jenny. Trixie and Seymour rose as soon as Bryan and Caroline walked through the doors. Henry Buttersample smiled as he watched a new batch of children enter his emporium.

Ralph hurried up to Elt and his dad. He eagerly offered his dad a piece of candy from his bag, and his father accepted. Ralph then took over the leash duties. Jenny followed suit and offered her mom a piece of candy as well. She bent down and hugged Bernadette. Caroline and Bryan walked up to Henry Buttersample and offered him a piece of candy from their bags. Henry laughed, then politely declined. "I only eat one piece a day," said Henry. "And I will do so at the end of the day, but thank you."

"Thank you for the terrific tour," said Caroline.

"Yeah, maybe we can give you a tour of the Observatory one day," mentioned Bryan. "It's where me dad works." Bryan gazed up at his father. Professor Greenlee smiled and nodded. "There's going to be a big announcement this week, right dad?" asked Bryan.

"Yes son," replied the professor.

"Then I'll be awaiting the exciting news," proclaimed Henry. "Thank you again for coming. If you're really good and do all of your chores at home, I'm sure that your parents will bring you back here real soon."

"You bet!" said Ralph.

The Greenlees, Eltisons, Rodgers, and their pets strolled across the street to Drexel's. Trixie and Seymour would now get to experience Drexel's Pet Store for the very first time. Elt and Bernadette would get to visit their old home once again, even though it had been only one night for Elt.

Inside the pet store, the children roamed the aisles with their pets, even aisles that weren't for dogs and cats. There was no place in town where folks could bring their pets inside, except for Drexel's. The kids took advantage of the air conditioning and the aisles stocked full of treats for their pets.

The Greenlees purchased new dog and cat beds for Trixie and Seymour, as well as some tasty treats for them. Elt and Bernadette both received their favorite; beef flavored doggie bones. As they headed toward their cars, the kids and pets said good-bye to each other.

"Hey," called Ralph to Bryan and Caroline. "Would you like to walk Trixie and Seymour with us sometimes?" The Greenlee children looked up at their parents.

"I can't see why not," answered Mrs. Greenlee.

"And as for the big announcement," added Professor Greenlee. "You'll soon be hearing some very exciting news about what's happening at the Observatory, but when the true event occurs, you all will be invited."

"Sounds great!" said Mr. Eltison.

Ms. Rodgers nodded in agreement. "Jenny and I will be there."

"We may go swimming later, want to come?" Jenny asked the Greenlee kids.

"Can we go Dad?" implored Bryan.

"Let's go home for some lunch," answered his dad, "and then you and Caroline can meet the children."

"We'll wait for you at my house," said Jenny.

So it was decided. Ralph, Jenny, Caroline, and Bryan polished off the perfect morning with swimming in the afternoon. The long day concluded with a short walk for Jenny, Ralph, Elt, and Bernadette. The Greenlee children would join them for a walk another day.

As the business day closed at seven o'clock that evening, Henry Buttersample wiped his brow, gazed at the clock in the lobby, and ushered out the last handful of customers. It had been a fantastic opening day, one that he and his family couldn't believe. They would work well into the night re-stocking their empty shelves, awaiting the next day's arrival of excited children and parents. As Henry began to lock his doors, he noticed a man approaching him.

"I'm afraid we're about to close sir," explained Henry. "But if you want to make a last second purchase, please...."

"Are you Henry Buttersample?" asked the mysterious man.

"Why yes I am," answered Henry. "How can I assist you?"

"You're the one that invented that new candy, aren't you?" asked the stranger.

"How did you...?" asked Henry.

"I represent a very wealthy businessman who is very interested in your new invention," answered the stranger. He moved closer to Henry. "May I have a moment of your time?"

The candy store owner stood there at the door, frozen for a moment. Then he stepped back and let the man in. Stunned, Henry locked the door, closed the shade, and switched the "Open" sign to "Closed."

CHAPTER 3

"READY TO TRY AGAIN?" ASKED Jasmine.

The super dog backed up on his roof as far as he could go. He then charged forward and leaped. It may have resembled a flying dog, but it was just the momentum from the leap off the roof that enabled Elt to land about twenty feet away from the house.

"I don't get it," muttered a dejected Elt. "Coladeus said that one day I would be able to fly."

Jasmine approached and consoled Elt. "Maybe you need a stronger magic stone."

It was night. Both Ralph and his dad, as well as all of the humans on Springhaven Court, were asleep. Although Ralph had become a lighter sleeper ever since the night Coladeus landed in his backyard, on some evenings, Elt was able to sneak out of the house. He would exit through the doggie door and freshen-up on his super skills.

Running and jumping were no issues. Elt continued to leap over the fence with ease. He would dash over to Valleydale Drive and back in mere seconds. Elt discovered new objects to lift, not just the old tree log in the backyard. He started with landscape rocks; the large ones in and around his and Jasmine's yards. He lifted the ends of parked cars, his doghouse - - whatever he could find. But the flying issue had bothered Elt. Coladeus promised that flying would be an eventual talent, yet Elt still hadn't mastered it. There was no way of contacting Coladeus; the Trianthian always contacted him first. There was no way Elt could ask him why he couldn't fly yet.

"Do you want to try one more time?" supported Jasmine.

Elt thought for a few seconds. He then dashed off in a flash and leaped. He soared pretty high, about eight feet, but then streamed back down. He trotted despondently back over to Jasmine. "I wanted to try something else, not from the roof, but it still didn't work."

"Still was pretty impressive," replied Jasmine.

"I think I'm going to head back inside," said a disappointed Elt. He started to head towards the back door. Jasmine followed, hoping to cheer him up.

"Sure you don't want to outrun some rabbits in my yard?" Jasmine tempted. Elt shook his head no and continued walking.

"Hey, do you think those two will make it to the meeting?" asked Jasmine.

"Bernadette and I managed it," answered Elt. "I will help them, but it's their job to make it outside."

What meeting were Elt and Jasmine referring to? To obtain that answer, we have to revisit the day Trixie and Seymour moved into the neighborhood.

After she had witnessed the arrival of the poodle and especially (for her) the new feline, Jasmine raced over to Sarge's house. The Boxer was lazily napping in his doghouse that hot summer afternoon. Jasmine jumped onto the fence, leaped down into Sarge's yard, and hurried over to his doghouse. "Wake up!" she cried.

The half-groggy Boxer slightly opened his eyes. "Go away," he yawned. "You're interrupting sleepy time."

"It's important," insisted the tabby cat.

Sarge mumbled, his eyes closing again. "Anyone in trouble? Dognapped or something?"

The tabby shook her head impatiently. She waited until she couldn't take it anymore, then she leaned over and shrieked right into his ear. "MEOW!"

Completely startled, the Boxer frantically scrambled up and banged his head on the overhang of the doghouse. "What is it? What's going on?" he gasped. He then fixed his attention on Jasmine, who sat quietly in the grass, innocently licking a paw. Sarge sighed, shrugged his shoulders and shook the pain out of his head, for he realized that it was only the tabby sitting there. "What do you want?" he demanded.

Jasmine continued grooming herself for a few seconds. "Oh, just wandering through the neighborhood, saw you sleeping, thought I'd wake you up, and oh, by the way, there are two new pets in the neighborhood," said Jasmine.

"Well, of course there are two new pets," replied Sarge impatiently. "Elt and Bernadette, everyone knows that."

"Two *newer* pets, and one of them is a cat," retorted Jasmine. "Not sure how I'm feeling about that yet."

"New pets? In our neighborhood? Where?" asked Sarge.

"Duh. Right across from you," answered Jasmine.

The Boxer paused for a second or two. "Oh, I saw that human's storage machine there earlier," realized Sarge. "Those two rascals must have slipped past me while I was closing my eyes."

"Well, are we going to have a meeting?" asked Jasmine. "You know, welcome them to the neighborhood?"

"Yes, of course we will," replied Sarge. "Set it up for the next full moon, but when the sun is at its highest, and at Juan's garage. Oh, and make sure he has plenty of those scrumptious biscuits."

"We have to hold the meeting when it's dark outside," reminded Jasmine.

"What? Why?"

"Because Elt's and Bernadette's young humans are home during the day now," replied Jasmine. "I'm sure Trixie's and Seymour's young ones are home, too."

"Trixie and C-Who?" asked the Boxer.

"The new pets," continued Jasmine. "And it's Seymour, the cat."

"Oh, I hate upsetting my human," sighed Sarge. "He hates leaving me outside now at night. This isn't going to be easy."

"We'll work it out," said a determined Jasmine. "I'll get Elt and Bernadette to help us."

"Ok, then. Gather up the troops, uh, *please*, and we'll have another meeting," instructed Sarge. So Jasmine slipped away and sped over to Juan's house. The Chihuahua was inside asleep, for it was siesta time on that hot summer afternoon. Like she did previously, Jasmine had to wait quite some time before Juan and Max ventured outside. Max and Juan would have to find a way to sneak out, like they did before, to attend the next meeting. Juan, of course, had his doggie door, but Mrs. Perez kept a closer eye on her baby since the day he went missing.

"Two new pets?" laughed Juan. "Hooray! I'm so happy that there is another pussycat."

"Haven't seen them yet," commented Max. "I guess we could hold another meeting, but at night, that's going to be tougher than before."

Max wandered over to the side of his yard. Max stood still and stared at the Greenlee's house.

"Didn't know new humans moved in," said Max. "Getting older means too many naps. They must have slipped past me."

"Ha. That's what Sarge said," smirked Jasmine.

So Max and Juan confirmed the neighborhood meeting with Jasmine. Juan loved to host the meetings, for his garage was always neat, clean, and full of dog biscuits.

Jasmine skipped Bernadette's house, for she would simply relay the message to Elt. He would then inform Bernadette during one of their walks together, or if he had to, on a nightly visit. The nightly visit would be difficult, especially if Bernadette was asleep. Elt would want no part of sticking his head through Bernadette's doggie door and attempting to wake the Cocker Spaniel up. Bernadette, like Elt, usually slept with her human.

Jasmine then dashed over to Mrs. Yao's house to visit Chin. Instead of meditating, the Chow Chow was walking through his yard, slowly, like tip-toeing. It was as if he was trying to walk lighter than air, for each step was a light, deliberate step.

"Better freshen up on your proverbs, Buddy," asserted Jasmine as she reached Chin. "Meeting at Juan's on the next full moon when the sky is dark." Even though Chin continued his odd walk undisturbed, Jasmine figured he had heard her, so she wasted no time. She leaped over Chin's fence, darted through her yard, stopped at her water bowl for a quick drink, and then headed over to Elt's house.

"Do you want to come with me to invite Trixie and Seymour?" asked Jasmine when she caught up with Elt.

"Sure," responded Elt. "But how do we know when they'll be outside alone?"

"We'll just have to stake out their business patterns," replied Jasmine. "Let's try to catch them both together when their humans let them outside. If not, we'll just have to tell one of them. We can start tonight, after your human falls asleep." Elt agreed and padded back into his house.

Jasmine's last stop was by Prince's house. Although he had lived in the neighborhood for a few years, Prince was actually the newest member of the group of pets that met in Juan's garage. It was dusk by the time Prince patrolled the yard; he took care of business on the same trip. Prince noticed the tabby perched on his fence. He didn't bother to chase her. "There are no rabbits here," declared Prince. "I believe I've chased them all away. Keeps me in excellent shape, you know."

"Not here for rabbits," replied Jasmine. "I just wanted to invite you to our next meeting."

"When is our appointment?" asked the Doberman.

The next full moon," answered Jasmine, "when our humans are asleep, just like the last time."

"What's on the agenda?"

"Nothing big. Just two new pets in the neighborhood … again."

"They'll let anyone in the neighborhood nowadays," remarked Prince. "My human locks the doors at night, though. He wants to make sure I stay inside."

"Find a way," instructed Jasmine as she leaped over the fence and scampered home.

Jasmine had once again organized a meeting and delivered messages to all of the neighborhood pets. Now came the difficult part; tracking down Trixie and Seymour. Elt and Jasmine would start scoping their new friends' business patterns, and then confront them one week later, when it was closer to the full moon. They would meet after Ralph and his dad were asleep. The only concern was that it might be too late, for if the Greenlees retired to bed early, then Trixie and Seymour would be inside, unaware that there was a welcoming committee just outside their door.

Elt had planned to rest briefly the night of the visit while Ralph fell asleep, then rendezvous with Jasmine. What Elt didn't count on was a sudden message crackling out of the transmitter on his collar. "Elt...Can you hear me?" Elt jerked awake and quickly crept out of the room, so as not to wake his human. He slipped enthusiastically through the doggie door onto his back porch. Thrilled, he replied, "Yes, I can hear you!"

"Elt, my friend, this is Coladeus. Are you alone? Is your human Ralph with you?"

"No, he is sleeping."

"Excellent," stated Coladeus. "Elt, a situation has arisen on one of our missions. We will need your assistance." What grogginess Elt had left, quickly disappeared. His eyes widened and he stood up on all fours. This is what he had been waiting for. Not that being Ralph's pet wasn't fulfilling enough, but he had been granted special powers. He wanted these powers to be used more often. "But I need to converse with you and your human, so he will know what is transpiring," added Coladeus. I will meet with you and your human, Ralph, in two nightfalls. Please be ready for my arrival." Elt agreed, and the transmission ended.

"But wait," insisted Elt. "What do you want me to do? Will I get to fly?" There was no response. In all of the excitement Elt forgot to ask those important questions. What was he going to do? Was he going to remain on Earth? Did Coladeus need the assistance of Jasmine or Bernadette?

"Are you ready?" asked a familiar voice. Jasmine strode over to the porch stairs to meet her friend.

"Yeah, I guess," answered Elt as he gazed up intently at the stars. Elt expected to witness the Trianthian ship pass by at that very moment.

"What is it?" asked Jasmine.

"I just received a transmission from Coladeus."

"Really?" The tabby was fascinated. "What's going on?"

"I don't know, but he wants both my human and me to meet him in two dark times," replied Elt. "Maybe I'm going with him on a mission." His eyes sparkled.

Jasmine jumped onto the back porch railing, incredulous. "Wow, you mean you might travel with the outer space guy?"

"Don't know," answered Elt.

"Do you think I can meet him? I've never met a being from outer space."

"Maybe you could hang out close by," suggested Elt. "So you can catch a glimpse, but not alarm him."

Jasmine thought for a few seconds. "Fair enough," she said. "So are you ready?"

"Yep."

The two trekked over to Valleydale Drive and stopped in front of the Greenlee's residence. Elt and Jasmine waited patiently as midnight approached. At last, the outside light turned on and the front door opened. First, Seymour ran out, then Trixie, and then the door closed. Whew. Having a human outside the door would have been quite a challenge for Elt and Jasmine.

Trixie ventured one way while Seymour pranced to the other side of the yard. The business of taking care of business required some privacy, plus there were many new places in the yard to discover, full of many exciting scents.

"You take Trixie and I'll find Seymour," directed Jasmine.

"No wait," cautioned Elt. "Let them take care of their ... you know what I mean. Then we'll catch them together before they go inside." So Elt and Jasmine jumped the fence quietly, not to be heard by either Greenlee pet. In mere moments, both Seymour and Trixie appeared from opposite sides of the yard, startled to discover Elt and Jasmine on their sidewalk leading to the front porch.

"What's the meaning of this intrusion?" snapped Seymour in his distinguished British accent. The standing hairs on Seymour's back began to ease down then, for he realized that his counterparts were not planning an attack. Trixie sat down, batted her eyes fashionably, and waited for an answer.

"Uh, we're from the Cat-Dog Neighborhood Welcoming Committee," started Jasmine. "And what better time, than on a really late night like tonight, can we say . . . welcome to the neighborhood! And by the way, you're both invited to our next meeting."

Seymour paused for a few seconds, glanced over at Trixie, and then fixed his attention back on Elt and Jasmine. "You're saying that you have a welcoming committee in this primitive community of yours?"

Jasmine edged closer to Elt. "What's 'primitive' mean?" she whispered. Elt wasn't paying any attention at all to the conversation. Once again, Elt was fixated on Trixie.

"I, I don't know," Elt stammered as he stared at the poodle. Jasmine had witnessed Elt's fascination with Trixie from afar that one day. Something needed to be done, but she wasn't as bold as Bernadette had been, barking at Elt to snap him out of his trance. Maybe a screeching, hair-raising 'meow' might have done the trick. But not then, not at night when they were all in front of the Greenlee's home. Jasmine just turned away from Elt.

"We meet once a full moon, but usually when the sun is way high in the sky," explained Jasmine. "This time we'll meet when it's dark, at Juan the Chihuahua's place, over there." Jasmine pointed in the direction of Juan's house. Trixie gazed over at Elt, then back at Seymour.

"Well, I do declare," voiced the Poodle. "We'd be honored to attend. We Greenlees have always attended the finest of galas, balls, and ceremonies."

"Well, it's not like that at all," Jasmine tried to clarify.

"Oh well Trixie, if you insist that we attend this obviously rash and uncivilized gathering, then I will make sure that I am groomed to perfection," announced Seymour. "However, it's been quite some time so my tongue will receive quite a workout."

"And I must undergo an appointment at the local groomer," interjected Trixie. Elt snapped out of his trance. He noticed a look of frustration on Jasmine's face.

"Look kids, it's not what you think," said Jasmine firmly. "We meet in a garage, though it's very clean. Juan lays out a bowl of dog treats, Sarge grumbles some words, Max grumbles some back at him, and

Chin leaves us with some words of wisdom that usually make no sense."
Trixie and Seymour stood there, silent.

"Then how should we prepare for this meeting?" asked Seymour.

"Dude, just be out here at the same time, three dark times away,"
answered Jasmine.

"Make sure your humans let you out a little early, so we can pick you
up," offered Elt, finally involved in the discussion. "We'll have to make
sure you get back before your humans go searching for you. That's kind
of happened to us before."

"Three evenings from this one. We will be prompt," pronounced
Seymour as he counted the claws on his paw. "Please be here to escort
us." Seymour turned around and headed up the front porch steps.

"Good bye Elt," twinkled Trixie as she curtsied before Elt and
Jasmine. When she reached the top step, Trixie looked back, but Elt
and Jasmine were gone. She turned back around and brushed her paw
up against the storm door. In mere seconds, the door opened, and
Trixie and Seymour walked inside. Professor Greenlee stuck his head
outside, shot a quick glance around, and then retreated, closing the door
behind him.

Elt and Jasmine had quickly exited the scene, but then slowly ambled
home. "Hey, what's up with you and that poodle?" purred Jasmine.

"What do you mean?"

"You're like in a trance or something, whenever she's around."

Elt admitted, "I think she's the most beautiful creature I've ever
seen."

"Oh boy. We'd better not let Bernadette hear that one," advised
Jasmine. With that, the two separated and headed to their respective
homes. Elt slipped through his doggie door, sipped some water from
his bowl, and crept into Ralph's bedroom.

Elt rested, thinking about the next couple of days. A meeting with
Coladeus in two days and a neighborhood meeting the day after. What
did Coladeus need? Where would he go? All he knew was that Ralph
had to be out there with him. Whatever it was, he would be very busy
for the next few days. He could be gone for a short time, for he might
just have to travel to another part of Earth, or he could be gone a very
long time, possibly to another planet. Would he miss the neighborhood

meeting? Either way, Elt figured that Spring Valley would be okay during his absence.

What Elt didn't realize was that Spring Valley was in for a big change, in fact a big change in time.

CHAPTER 4

"THE FASCINATION OF TIME TRAVEL has enthralled many of man's most intelligent minds," the speaker told his audience. "H.G. Wells wrote about it, and there are scores of movies and television programs devoted to the subject of time travel." The audience in the observatory's auditorium sat silently, fixed upon the words of the speaker. Not one seat was empty.

The speaker paused for a few seconds, picked up a handkerchief from his podium, and methodically dabbed his brow. It was the middle of summer, and the air conditioning wasn't cooling the auditorium well. He then took a sip of water from a glass that was also situated on the podium.

The speaker was no ordinary speaker. Not only was he Spring Valley's most notable scientist, he was one of the greater region's most scientific minds. His experiments in science were recognized as some of the most intelligent and thorough in the entire world. The speaker was none other than Professor Eric Van Hausen, whose observatory and campus encompassed about three square miles of buildings, satellites, and warehouses. One old warehouse, of course, was rented to the infamous Walter Eugene Crum and his band of miscreants. Van Hausen was an honorable man, and in no way would have knowingly rented his warehouse to any unscrupulous character of whom he could have suspected foul play.

Clad in his white lab coat, his hair long, wavy, and a bit disheveled, the professor finished his sip of water and gazed intensely at his audience. His eyes were glazed with passion, his posture stern and un-wavering. "Those who have studied with and under me, know that I have a little bit of interest in time travel." The crowd laughed. Everyone on campus knew of the professor's deep passion for time travel.

"My fascination stems from when I was a lad reading science-fiction comic books," revealed Professor Van Hausen. "As I matured, my interest grew more and more. I attended seminars, science-fiction conventions, and even met with prolific authors whose stories mainly dealt with the subject of time travel."

The Professor paused a moment to give his next statement the weight it deserved. "Through many years, countless experiments, and exorbitant expenses," he paused, "I believe that I have discovered a way to actually travel through time."

The audience gasped. Some clapped in wonder. Some cheered. A majority of the group were students, co-workers, and colleagues of the professor. Many of these folks knew of the professor's obsession with time travel, but never dreamed even his brilliant mind could make it a reality. The crowd in the sold out auditorium included writers and photographers from the Herald Newspaper. Surely after the announcement, the news of time travel would hit every corner of the planet. Spring Valley would be one of the most important and recognized towns in the world!

"I, I mean we, my associates and myself, have devised an extraordinary device," declared Professor Van Hausen. The professor turned around and politely gestured to the two associates standing behind him, also wearing white laboratory coats. One man was tall and thin, the other, short and medium-built. The tall man was Professor Stanley Greenlee, the other associate was Edward B. Livingstone.

Edward Boris Livingstone had been a student of Van Hausen's many years ago. The teacher admired the young student, for he studied hard and worked diligently. And, of course, he had intriguing thoughts on time travel. When Edward was finished with his studies on campus, he was hired as Eric's Personal Executive Assistant. Wherever Professor Van Hausen went, Edward Livingstone was either right by the professor's side or shortly behind. In fact, he had stood beside the professor through lean and tough times for nearly thirty years. He was the professor's strictest confidant. He was a friend, a partner, and a fellow time traveling enthusiast. But then one day a stranger walked into Van Hausen's life, and became the one key ingredient to the professor's dreams and visions. His name was Professor Stanley Greenlee.

Long before Eric Van Hausen met Greenlee, however, the professor had meddled with time travel experiments. He had consulted the highest authorities from around the globe. He had constructed various prototypes of time machine devices; they were primitive, but they were the first of their kind. When the experiments were successful, then modifications would be established.

For over twenty years, the professor and Edward floundered in many failed experiments. Although he expended millions of dollars on these failed attempts, his observatory, college of sciences, and science labs flourished. Professor Van Hausen chose the right people to manage his business, and it grew. Eric started out with two small buildings: his laboratory, and his offices. Thirty years later, Observatory Road was lined for two miles with structures, facilities, and satellite dishes dedicated to the advancement of space studies and science research.

Folks from Spring Valley knew Professor Van Hausen. Although they knew he was a bit eccentric and a little cuckoo about the subject of time travel, Spring Valley benefited from the professor's successes. His good business practices created new jobs in the town and more folks wanting to move to Spring Valley because of the success of the observatory.

As the fascination with time travel became more of an obsession, however, the observatory began to feel the effects of the professor's reluctance to cut back on experimental expenses. Repairs that were needed to update all of the computers and equipment were either delayed or disregarded. The overall state of the observatory's facilities was in deep disrepair. In fact, on this, the very day of the professor's speech, there was a reason why it was so hot in the auditorium. The air conditioning was on the fritz and desperately needed replacement.

About eight months before this evening, just about the time the professor had begun contemplating defeat on the idea of a time machine, Professor Stanley Greenlee walked into his life. The professor was teaching physics when he noticed a tall, slender man sitting quietly in the second row, jotting down a note or two every few minutes. He knew that it wasn't one of his students, but he didn't mind the visitor. Now there had been times when special guests had walked in and listened to one of Van Hausen's lectures, but they usually sat down in the back of the hall, not to draw any attention away from the speaker.

When the class was finished, the mysterious man approached Professor Van Hausen. "Excuse me sir." He had a very polite British accent. Professor Van Hausen was erasing the notes he had scribbled on the blackboard. He turned around to face the visitor. "Allow me to introduce myself," continued the likeable guest. "My name is Greenlee. Professor Stanley Greenlee. I have traveled across the Atlantic to speak with you about an important matter." Stanley held out his hand. The professor politely shook it.

"And to what do I owe the pleasure this fine afternoon?" asked Professor Van Hausen. "I have another appointment today and am afraid my time is limited." Stanley smiled, for he knew that the professor was a busy man and didn't really have the time for conversation.

"I'm elated that you mentioned the word 'time,' for that is why I am here," related Stanley. "I have a few ideas to discuss with you concerning your travels into the past and future." That's all Stanley needed to say, because frankly, that's all Van Hausen needed to hear. The man in front of him could have known absolutely nothing about the subject in reality, but the professor was at the brink of desperation.

The plain fact of it all was that although he felt he had come close, without the key components needed to make it operational, Eric Van Hausen, after all those years, had failed to create a functional time machine. The complex ideas he and Edward had attempted to develop had failed. The failures were complex too; there were many different facets of each equation. An adjustment of time codes solved one issue, but then other issues would raise their ugly heads.

Now there have been many theories concerning time travel and the use of a time machine. Scientists involved with these theories were called physicists. Many physicists believed that in order to go back in time, one would have to travel with bolting speed in reverse around the Earth a certain number of cycles, depending on how far back in time the traveler wanted to venture. With the intense speeds and a power source needed to generate that speed, the time machine would literally "disappear" and travel through a parallel universe in time.

In theory, it sounded plausible, but in reality, it wasn't possible. Or was it? Many time travel researchers believed that there were already time travelers on Earth, in disguise, blending in with the humans they surrounded themselves with.

What did Professor Van Hausen believe? Well, being obsessed with the whole subject matter of time travel and time machines, the professor was pretty much open to any idea. But there was one thing holding him back. If there were time travelers, then where were the time machines and why didn't he know about them? With all of his soul, Professor Eric Van Hausen wanted to be the one honored scientist to invent a perfectly functional time machine.

"I am free in the morning," smiled Professor Van Hausen. "Are you able to stop by?"

"Certainly." The conversation ended pleasantly. Van Hausen scribbled the directions to his facility onto a piece of paper and handed it to Stanley.

"Professor, until we meet again."

"Ah. See you in the morning, Professor."

It was a restless evening for the two professors, for they both ignored sleep, preparing their notes and formulas for the next day's meeting. Stanley was excited about working with a professor from the United States. Van Hausen hoped this young British professor had some insight into where he and Edward had gone wrong.

When morning arrived, both men woke up and prepared themselves for the day, packed up their notes, and headed to their destination. Stanley arrived promptly at eight o'clock, with Professor Van Hausen already there to greet him. Stepping inside the laboratory, Greenlee's jaw almost dropped when he witnessed the view before him.

Behind a couple of long wooden desks covered with papers, tools, and test tubes, stood a mechanical wonder about eight feet in height, and ten feet in length. It was girded with steel bracings and thick, plastic windows. It sparkled with dozens of colored lights, much like a fully decorated Christmas tree. The entry door was situated inside a metal frame on the right side. The machine was equipped for up to four travelers: two in the front seat, and two in the back. Its platform was round and could rotate at very high speeds. A fan whirred somewhere under the machine, presumably to prevent it from overheating.

Professor Greenlee stood motionless for a moment or two. He approached the time machine and stood in awe at what he felt was a masterpiece waiting for its trial run. Van Hausen paused beside him to admire his work of nearly thirty years. Professor Greenlee wandered over to a nearby chalkboard and scanned the countless equations that were crowded there. "Is this your formula for the relativity of time and space?" breathed Professor Greenlee.

"Why, yes. Yes it is," beamed Professor Van Hausen.

Professor Greenlee studied the board silently for at least five minutes. He was a master of formulas. At Oxford University, where he both studied and taught, the professor was known to engage in formula calculating for days without coming out of his office. Greenlee touched the board with his fingers. He took a deep breath. "Professor, what are you utilizing as your power source, and what functions as your time and space converter?"

Professor Van Hausen motioned for Stanley to join him as he moved closer to the time machine console display unit. On the unit were dozens of buttons, switches, and lights. Van Hausen pointed to a series of blinking lights encased in a framed gray box on the console. On top of the console were a series of four lighted test-tube like bulbs that emitted a kind of energy within the glass. "This is my Quantum Module Facilitator," answered Professor Van Hausen with satisfaction. "It was, and I hope still is, my answer to the mystery of time travel."

Professor Greenlee examined the mechanism carefully. "And it regulates the power needed to make the jump from space to time?"

"Precisely," answered Van Hausen. He then pointed to a sizeable gray canister situated against the wall, next to the console. Attached to the can was a series of thick gray cords that were connected to a junction box on the time machine platform. On that box was a red dial, presumably a power starter. "Here is the main power transformer. It has plenty of holding power; enough gigawatt potential to sustain the mightiest of thrusts.

"So lack of power is not an issue?" inquired Professor Greenlee.

"No. The key to traveling in time is somewhere in these formulas."

"Then can we get started?" asked a smiling Professor Greenlee.

"There is no better time!

And so it began. Professor Van Hausen canceled all appointments that day. In fact, he re-scheduled all appointments, activities, and classes for the entire week. He had attempted everything. He had formulated scores of theories. He needed a new perspective, a new approach. Eric Van Hausen truly believed that this man, whom he had met only the day before, likely held the crucial clue, the final answer.

The two men worked feverishly. No lunch. No dinner. They traded values, formulas, and theories. When Edward Livingstone, Eric Van Hausen's personal assistant, walked into the room later that day, he was shocked to find another man at the professor's side. It had always been him. He didn't know what to say.

The work continued well into the night. Edward attempted to assist, but found himself the odd man out. It was inconceivable. It was as if the professor had forgotten about all the hard work they had accomplished together. Sometime past midnight, the two professors decided that they would resume in the morning. Edward asked if he would be needed. Van Hausen told him to come in to complete some paperwork while he and the professor continued their research.

The next morning, Van Hausen offered Greenlee a position as his Senior Executive Assistant. Edward was just his Executive Assistant. The offer was for a permanent stay, not just to initiate the time machine project. Greenlee would receive a rather lucrative salary, even though money was scarce at the observatory and Van Hausen wasn't quite sure how he was going to swing it. Professor Greenlee accepted the position and the two professors shook hands that very morning to seal the deal. Professor Van Hausen also offered his new employee a furnished on-campus apartment. Professor Greenlee kindly accepted, and moved in later that day.

"I am married to a wonderful lady and have two delightful children," said Greenlee to his new partner. "At some point after we get this time machine functional, I will bring them over to the States."

"Wonderful," smiled Van Hausen. "We're so close, I feel certain now that this time machine will be a reality. I can't wait to meet your family." Professor Van Hausen sensed that this new brilliant mind would be the one to find the missing piece to the puzzle, the reason why he couldn't fully operate the time machine.

The town of Spring Valley experienced their worst snowstorm in history on that New Year's Day, but Greenlee and Van Hausen paid no attention to the weather outside. Their only concern was for the power to remain on, so that they could continue their work. They did possess a generator, but it would limit their capabilities when it pertained to experiments they needed to conduct. Luckily for them, the professors never lost power.

Two weeks later, Professor Greenlee finally cracked the code, and discovered the missing clue. "What we need is in this chip." Professor Greenlee held up a small computer chip in his right hand.

"Yes, go on. Please." Van Hausen's eyes were wide.

"On this chip we will conjugate formulas for traveling both forward and backward in time, while also commanding signals that determine the travel and time conversion rates," explained Professor Greenlee.

"Yes. Edward and I formulated a chip before, but we couldn't get the chip to perform its function."

"Then may I?" asked Greenlee.

"By all means," allowed Van Hausen cheerfully. "I'm very interested in where your calculations take you." So Greenlee sequestered himself in the corner of the room, at a small desk, using a notebook, scientific calculator, and his small laptop computer. Professor Van Hausen offered assistance, but Greenlee politely declined.

A week later, Professor Van Hausen entered his laboratory and was startled to find Professor Greenlee placing a computer chip into a module of the time machine. Greenlee looked up with exhausted eyes filled with excitement. "Pardon me for my being here early and not telling you, but I wanted to set up everything before you arrived." Van Hausen paused for only a moment, and then hastened towards the machine platform and console. "I think we have something," grinned Stanley, hardly able to contain himself.

"You mean?" asked a startled Professor Van Hausen. Stanley Greenlee walked out of the machine and over to the console. He switched the main power to "on."

"Where and when do you want to go?" Stanley rubbed his hands together.

The professor was speechless. He had dreamed about this moment, but never imagined it would actually occur. "I don't know," he finally stuttered. "There are so many places I'd like to see, both in the future and in the past."

"Sir, this is just a test," reminded Greenlee. "Just like the hundreds of tests you've already conducted. But something tells me that this time it's going to work. Just make the destination a simple one."

"I could visit Caesar in Rome, or watch the pyramids being constructed," declared Professor Van Hausen. "But not yet. Yes, keep it simple." Van Hausen gazed at the console before him. "Set the date to September 22, 1975."

"Why that date?" asked Stanley.

"That's the day it all began on this very spot. And bring me back in fifteen minutes."

Greenlee set the coordinates on the console. Professor Van Hausen skipped up to the platform and stepped inside the time machine. He looked out at Stanley as he sat down, fastened his safety belt, and donned his oxygen mask.

The professors paused a moment as their eager eyes met and full smiles lit their faces. They nodded to each other. This was a moment that would change history forever. Professor Greenlee pushed a few more buttons on the console. The motor thrummed and the time machine began to slowly rotate on its platform. After a few more touches on the board, the time machine began to spin round and round, faster and faster. Greenlee was amazed at its beauty. Could it really work? Now the time machine was only a blur, and the professor inside could hardly be seen. Then suddenly, a deafening BLAM shook the walls, a blast of light from the central power unit ripped across the room, and then there was smoke. Billows and billows of smoke. When the smoke cleared, the time machine was gone.

Stanley blinked, paused for a few moments, and then moved quickly to where the time machine had been. He grinned, elated. Had it worked? Had they succeeded?

Meanwhile, Van Hausen witnessed what he thought was a dream. He saw flashing lights, reverse rotations around the Earth, and brief scenes of history flash before him. Then everything stopped, stark and sudden. The professor had landed.

The smoke inside the cabin cleared, and Van Hausen unfastened his seatbelt. He rose slowly and stretched his knees, for his legs were weak from the force of the trip. He hesitated by the door for a long moment, a hundred questions swirling in his mind. Then he gingerly pushed it open. What he saw filled him with wonder and awe. It had worked! The time machine was a success!

The professor checked his watch. Only a couple of minutes had passed. But when he stepped out of the time machine, he was in the middle of a giant field, lined with a scattering of trees. A dirt road led off into the empty distance. There was one small building across the field and he knew what that structure was, for he had seen it before. The professor was standing where it had all started. On September 22, 1975, the professor had purchased the land, including that very building, and his science lab and observatory became a reality. He stood in this very field that would one day be his laboratory.

"Absolutely remarkable," whispered Van Hausen. "We did it."

The professor strode over to the dirt road. There was no one around. He knew he didn't have much time, as his fifteen minutes would soon be up. He would have to venture later. His next trip would be one to the past, to a place like Egypt or Rome.

Van Hausen checked his watch again and took one last look all around. Then he ducked back inside the time machine, buckled himself in, and awaited his return back to the laboratory. He couldn't believe it. Everything had worked as planned. His dream had become a reality. Since the time machine was in the middle of the field and there was no one in the building yet, the professor was quite sure that no one had seen him. Time traveling could be perilous for many reasons. Not only was it dangerous to travel in the time machine itself, but there was always a chance of being noticed. That one brief moment, especially if there was some kind of interaction, could re-alter history.

It was time. The machine began to hum and rotate. The hum increased, and the machine rotated faster and faster as it was lifted into the air. When it reached its maximum speed, the time machine disappeared with a flash and a bang and re-entered the normal Earth time pattern.

Stanley's eyes gleamed wide when the time machine suddenly reappeared in the lab. The machine's rotations were decreasing and the engine noise was slowing. Finally, the time machine came to a complete stop.

Professor Van Hausen kept his eyes closed for a moment, for all of the spinning made him quite dizzy. But then he unbuckled his seatbelt, and rose quickly from his seat. He flung open the door and stepped out into the steam spewing up from the bottom of the machine.

"Did you find what you were looking for on September 22, 1975?" shouted Greenlee hopefully.

The professor beamed and clasped his hands above his head like a prize fighter. "We have so much to do," he called. He rushed across the room and scanned the readings on the console. He ran back over to Stanley and read the notes on his clipboard. "We will need to market this discovery!"

"What was it like?" asked Stanley. "What did you see?"

Van Hausen stopped and clasped Stanley's right hand with his own, pumping it up and down. "Professor Greenlee, my dear friend and fellow time traveler, find a home for yourself and your family. You will be working here for a long time."

*   *   *

"So we will embark on a few more test trip experiments," continued Eric Van Hausen to the people in the hot auditorium. "If everything goes accordingly, then we will conduct a live time travel experience for everyone to witness."

The crowd applauded and cheered. They were ecstatic. Time travel? Really? It was unbelievable, but true. As the crowd continued to applaud, flash bulbs from the cameras lit up the podium area. The reporters from the Herald and the television stations wanted more information. Professor Van Hausen answered as many questions as he could. The euphoria in the auditorium had reached a peak but was still rising. As folks filed out of the auditorium, the buzz was endless.

The overall attitude on campus was one of joy and excitement; however, there was one individual who was not overjoyed. Alone in his apartment on campus later that afternoon, Edward B. Livingstone stared at a framed portrait of himself with Professor Van Hausen. "I helped the professor all those years," Livingstone glowered. "I'm the one who should be traveling in the time machine with him, not that goodie goodie know-it-all Greenlee guy."

Livingstone became more upset by the minute. He picked up a pencil and slowly tapped his temple with it. He had a plan. He was going to get even. "If I can't travel on that time machine, then neither will Greenlee," he vowed. Turning on his lamp, Livingstone started writing notes to himself on a piece of paper. He smiled deviously. "I'll get even with them. I'll get even with them both."

CHAPTER 5

"ELT, ELT, CAN YOU HEAR me?" pleaded the strange yet familiar voice on Elt's transmitter. Elt had just dozed off next to his human. "Elt, this is Coladeus, can you hear me?" Both Mr. Eltison and Ralph were asleep, so Elt rose slowly and entered the dining room. "I'm here and ready," he said with quiet eagerness.

"Excellent," stated Coladeus. "We are orbiting Earth and I am about to board my space pod. I shall be visiting you and your human Ralph in about fifteen of your Earth minutes."

"I understand," replied Elt. "I will go wake up my human." Elt padded back to Ralph's bedroom. He stood over his human and began to lick his face softly. Ralph just smiled in his sleep, for he enjoyed the affection from his dog. Elt would have to be a little more forceful to wake his sleeping human, but not too loud to awaken Mr. Eltison. Soon Ralph's face was covered with wet doggie kisses. Ralph opened his eyes and stretched. Elt jumped off the bed and stopped at the bedroom doorway, looking back expectantly. Ralph rose and propped himself up with his hands.

"What is it boy?" asked Ralph. Elt leaped back onto the bed and licked Ralph a couple of times, and then returned to the doorway, wagging. Remaining quiet, for he didn't want to awaken his dad, Ralph rose from his bed and followed Elt toward the kitchen. Elt zipped through his doggie door while Ralph unlocked and then opened the kitchen door and headed outside. Soon they both were standing under the weeping willow tree, next to Elt's doghouse.

Elt sat down and stared up at the sky. Ralph's drowsiness suddenly vanished as he realized what was happening. He and Elt were about to receive a visit from Coladeus! Ralph and Elt now both gazed up at the star-filled sky. It had been a hot day, but August nights in Spring Valley were cooler. Ralph shivered a bit. All of a sudden, they both witnessed a movement in the sky. It wasn't a plane, for a plane possessed lights and moved horizontally. The movement resembled a shadow in the night, moving closer and closer to them. They both knew who it was. Ralph took a deep breath and Elt wagged his tail.

The low hum of the egg-shaped pod became audible. Elt and Ralph backed away just a little to give Coladeus plenty of room to land. It was the first time Ralph had actually witnessed the landing of the Trianthian pod, although Ralph had seen it ascend only a short time ago. The pod slowly glided down and landed in front of the boy and his dog. A puff of steam billowed out from the bottom of the pod. Both Ralph's and Elt's eyes grew wider in anticipation of Coladeus's appearance.

Something big, something important was about to happen. Was Ralph going to be part of the adventure? Like in his daydreams, Ralph yearned to fly in some sort of a Trianthian space vessel; whether it was the space pod, or spaceship, Ralph didn't care. He just wanted to go. But how could he? How could he just disappear and fly away? His dad would wake up and worry. Would the trip to outer space be worth it? Was it safe? Questions and thoughts spun through Ralph's mind.

The door to the pod opened then, with more steam following. Coladeus emerged, stepped out onto the grass, adjusted his distransulator, and then approached Ralph and Elt. "So good to see you again Ralph," said Coladeus warmly.

Although he had met the alien before, Ralph was struck with awe so that he resembled someone in a trance. Staring straight at the Trianthian,

Ralph slowly raised his hand in order to shake Coladeus's four-fingered hand. Coladeus then moved over to Elt. He didn't say a word to Elt, but held out his hand. Elt promptly raised his right paw and they shook.

"I'm afraid I'm short on time this evening, my friend," stated the Trianthian, moving back over to Ralph. "The purpose of our meeting tonight is quite simple. I've come to ask a favor from you and Elt." Ralph heard the words emanating from Coladeus's mouth, but they weren't sinking in, not just yet. "A situation has arisen that needs our attention," continued Coladeus. "I need to borrow Elt for a short time to serve on a mission." Ralph didn't hear the words at first, not because Coladeus's distranslator wasn't functioning correctly, but just because he was still in awe from the whole encounter. "Does my need for Elt meet your approval, Ralph?" asked Coladeus.

Finally the words registered. Ralph shook his head and cleared his throat. "What will he be doing?" asked Ralph.

Since Ralph and Coladeus were basically the same height, the Trianthian didn't have to bend down to speak with the young human. Coladeus stared right into the boy's eyes and smiled. "Let's just say that his skills are required for this mission."

"Will. . .will it be dangerous?" asked Ralph. "Will I see Elt again? How long will he be gone?"

"It will be for a very short time, maybe a day or two in your Earth time," reassured Coladeus. "Every mission has some element of danger, but I'm quite sure that you will have Elt back safe and sound."

Ralph thought long and hard for a few seconds. The awe had worn off and reality had set in. His dog was leaving him again. It was not that long ago when Elt had disappeared for several days. Ralph was lonely and miserable. What was he going to do without his Elt?

"Can I be part of the mission?" asked Ralph hopefully.

"You are part of this mission," answered Coladeus.

"I am?" Ralph brightened. "How? And how can Elt be missing? My dad will see that he's not around."

"Exactly," replied Coladeus. "That's your part of the mission." Now Ralph was confused. Coladeus glanced back at the pod and snapped his alien fingers. The snap was a mild, yet distinctive sound. In mere seconds, another being exited from the space pod.

The being, another alien of some sort, was short and brown, and didn't glow. In fact, it was very difficult to see, for in the dark, only a faint outline of its body could be detected. Its eyes, though, were bright and white. The alien walked slowly out from the pod, stopped briefly to take a whiff of Elt, and then moved over beside the Trianthian. Elt returned a sniff, but felt no danger from the alien's presence. "This is Oleo, from the planet Sorg," announced Coladeus softly.

Oleo, who stood on two legs and possessed arms like those of a human, was hairy all over. In some ways Oleo resembled a small ape. He walked away from Coladeus and nuzzled up against Elt.

"Is he your friend?" inquired Ralph.

"I wouldn't say 'friend,'" answered Coladeus. "More like an agent, just as Elt is one of our agents." Coladeus reached over to Elt, switched his distranslator to canine speak, and spoke to Elt in what sounded like alien gibberish to Ralph. Coladeus then opened his pouch and pulled out a small object resembling a flashlight. He directed the object's light around the outline of Elt's body. He then shone the light around Oleo's entire body. What happened next blew Ralph's mind.

Even in the darkness, Ralph could witness the transformation. There wasn't any noise; not really any light, either. But Ralph watched it all by the greenish glow radiating off of Coladeus. In just under thirty seconds, Oleo's entire physical structure had changed. He now resembled. . .Elt. He was an exact duplicate!

Ralph couldn't believe it. Moments before, Oleo had been a two-legged, upright creature. Now it was a four-legged canine. If he didn't know where the real Elt was sitting, he would have had trouble figuring out who was who.

Ralph kneeled down in front of the replicate Elt. Coladeus re-adjusted his distranslator and looked at Ralph. "Proceed by giving him a command."

Ralph glanced at Coladeus, then back to the replicate. "Shake hands boy," commanded Ralph as he held out his right hand. Oleo raised its right paw and shook hands with Ralph. "Now your left," stated Ralph. Oleo raised its left paw and shook hands.

"He will understand your commands," instructed Coladeus. "It's all part of the transformation into Elt."

"Is he some kind of robot or computer?" asked Ralph.

"No, I discovered Oleo and a few of his kind on the planet Sorg three duraceps ago," explained Coladeus. He doesn't have any super powers like Elt, but as you can see, his talents are an asset."

"He can be anything he wants to?" asked Ralph.

"With a little assistance of Trianthian technology," grinned Coladeus as he held out the small metal object.

"So my whole job is to act like normal, and pretend Oleo is Elt." Ralph's flat statement hinted at his disappointment.

"Precisely," encouraged Coladeus. "I know it doesn't sound important, but it is. If Oleo can replicate Elt for a couple of your Earth days or so, then Elt and our team can complete the mission. So Ralph, you can see, we need you to assist us."

"Wow, I didn't think of it that way," said Ralph.

Coladeus started back for the pod. "We must be on our way. Thank you for allowing Elt to embark on the mission." Ralph bent down and hugged Elt. He thought of the danger in every mission, and how he had lost Elt once not too long ago. But this time it would only be for a couple of days and then Elt would return. Ralph should see him real soon.

After their embrace, Coladeus motioned for Elt to follow him, and Elt did. Ralph started to tear up, but he held the teardrops in, for he knew that his dog was embarking on a heroic mission. He also knew that he, Ralph Eltison, would be part of that mission. He had to keep himself together. Elt and Coladeus disappeared into the egg-shaped pod, but then Coladeus stuck his head out one more time.

"Please make sure to carry on a normal daily routine," cautioned the Trianthian. "Do with Oleo as you would do with Elt."

"So I should take him for walks like normal?" asked Ralph.

"Precisely," answered Coladeus. "Oleo learns fast, although I'm not sure how well he'll communicate with other canines." With that final mixed message, Coladeus ducked back inside and the door to the pod swung closed.

As the thrusters ignited and the pod jettisoned upward, Ralph weakly waved bye to Coladeus and Elt. The meeting with the alien had been exciting, but also disheartening, for his dog had left. Although he glanced down and saw Elt beside him, he knew that it wasn't really Elt.

Ralph had no way of communicating with Coladeus. Why couldn't he have his own transmitter stone thing too?

Ralph and Oleo watched as the pod disappeared into the stars. Then Ralph turned around and ambled back into the house. His new friend followed him. Ralph closed the door on Oleo, squatted, and stuck his head back through the doggie flap. Oleo picked up on the clue, and the new Elt entered the kitchen through the doggie door.

Ralph's 'new' pet followed him through the hallway, and into his bedroom, fervently sniffing everything, for he had to become familiar with his surroundings and quickly. Ralph pointed to the bed, and then collapsed onto it himself. The new Elt, who had already followed directions pretty well, leaped onto the bed, curled up on the edge, and rested. He didn't close his eyes, but kept his attention on Ralph.

Trying to digest all that had just occurred, Ralph closed his eyes and took a deep breath. Next, he opened one eye to see what the new Elt was doing. The dog had his head down, but his eyes were still wide open. Evidently, Sorgians didn't sleep much or required very little rest. Oleo stayed in his place, and Ralph eventually fell fast asleep.

Meanwhile, an exciting adventure was unfolding for Elt on board the pod, as Coladeus and Elt sped across Earth's atmosphere. The Trianthian pushed a selection of blinking buttons on his console. One of the buttons was some type of gravity feature, for both Elt and Coladeus, although strapped, didn't rise an inch in their seats. There were no objects floating around in the pod, either.

Elt's view of Earth was astounding. The blue of the oceans sparkled, while the green of the land was vivid. Elt realized he was leaving Earth, but was more interested in where he was headed. Elt watched Coladeus as he continued to monitor the keys and buttons on the console. His illumination created a greenish glow throughout the room.

All of a sudden, through the space pod window, Trianthius I appeared. Like its inhabitants, the triangular vessel's greenish glow shimmered against space's vast black canvas. As the pod drew closer to Trianthius I, a bay door opened on the mother ship, just like in Ralph's daydream. The pod spun its way to the much larger vessel. As it reached the doorway, the pod simply slowed and landed on a platform. Then the bay doors to Trianthius I closed.

"We're on board Trianthius I," announced Coladeus as he freed himself of his restraints. He reached over to unfasten Elt's, but the pooch had unfastened the seatbelt with his mouth. "Impressive," affirmed Coladeus. Elt was in total awe. He could have never imagined this. He was on board a real alien spaceship!

The pod hatch opened. Elt didn't know what to expect. Coladeus stood, and Elt stepped down off of his seat. The two walked out of the pod and onto the spaceship floor. The light in the room was faint, but everywhere a Trianthian stood or walked, a green hew illuminated that area.

Elt followed Coladeus down a long hallway that led to an elevator. The Trianthian leader pushed a series of buttons and the elevator door opened. Elt asked no questions, but just kept on following, for he sensed that right then was not the time. He figured his purpose for being there would be revealed soon. A moment later the elevator stopped. The door opened. They had reached the control room, better known as the "bridge" of the ship. Coladeus sat down on his captain's chair. He didn't speak into his distransulator. "My crew, this is Elt from Earth."

A Trianthian crewmember walked up to Elt and adjusted his vocal language device. "So this is the famous canine from Earth named Elt," stated the Trianthian. Elt paused. Strangely, he understood what the alien had just said.

"Elt, may I present Matheun, our First Officer," announced the alien. Elt approached Matheun and held up his right paw. Matheun adjusted his voice machine, but Elt spoke first.

"I am honored to be a guest on your awesome space transport machine."

Matheun shook Elt's paw. "It's called Trianthius I. It's our spaceship. Has the Captain briefed you on any part of your mission yet?" Elt shook his head no. "Then we must get started," directed Matheun. "Follow me." Elt glanced back at Coladeus, who remained seated in his chair, reviewing some notes on the computer screen in front of him.

The elevator door opened and Matheun stepped inside. "It's time to meet your team," remarked the first officer.

Elt followed. "Team?" he asked.

"You didn't expect to complete the mission on your own?" smiled Matheun. He pushed a couple of buttons on the elevator, and the door whisked closed. They now headed downward, but very quickly, the elevator stopped and the door opened again. It was dark.

"Second level. Our briefing room is straight ahead," informed Matheun. The first officer and Elt stepped off together, but Elt paused with a question.

"What is it?" asked Matheun.

"Will I be able to fly on this mission?" asked the super dog.

"I'm not sure," answered Matheun. "Did you ask the Captain?"

Elt shook his head no. "I was afraid that I wasn't doing something right."

Matheun reached over and twisted Elt's collar. "Maybe the captain needs to issue you an upgrade."

"An upgrade?"

"A bigger stone," clarified Matheun. Elt nodded. The two continued toward the briefing room door. This room was mainly used by Coladeus when holding meetings, but sometimes the room was used as a "relaxing area" for the crew. "Are you ready to meet your team?" coaxed Matheun.

Matheun opened the door. The room was brighter than the rest of the ship. Elt blinked, and then widened his eyes at the sight before him. He didn't know what the mission entailed, but there in front of him was his team. Elt followed the first officer inside and Matheun shut the door.

CHAPTER 6

RALPH AWAKENED THE NEXT MORNING the same way he fell asleep the night before. There were no kisses from his dog. When Ralph opened his eyes, the new Elt was staring at him just the way he had started before the boy fell asleep. Did Oleo ever go to sleep? Did Sorgians need sleep? It was just plain weird.

It had been around eight hours since Elt's departure, and Ralph already couldn't wait for Elt's return. The canine in front of him sure resembled his dog, but it wasn't. Ralph rose and stretched out of his bed. After a short trip to the restroom, he headed into the kitchen. The new Elt followed him slowly.

Ralph opened the pantry door and grabbed the bag of dog food. He dumped some dry food into Elt's dish. The new Elt hesitated, then moved over to the bowl and sniffed. He bit into a piece, tasted it, and then spit it out. Ralph laughed for a few seconds. "I guess you don't like dog food, huh?" Ralph said softly.

Ralph's dad walked into the kitchen. "Hey guys, do you want some eggs for breakfast this morning?"

"No thanks Dad, I think I'm gonna have a bowl of cereal today," answered Ralph.

Ralph's dad gazed at the dog standing by his food bowl. "What's the matter with Elt? Is he feeling okay?"

"I don't know," replied Ralph. "He doesn't seem hungry."

"Hmm. Something must be wrong," remarked Mr. Eltison. "Elt never went out and retrieved the newspaper."

Ralph almost smacked himself on the forehead. He totally forgot about the newspaper. Oleo had no idea that Elt retrieved the Herald newspaper in the rain, snow, or sunshine, every day, and delivered it to Mr. Eltison usually before Ralph's dad began his day. "I guess a walk later today might do him some good," recovered Ralph.

"Perhaps it would," commented Mr. Eltison. "Fresh air is always a great remedy when you're not feeling well."

"I'll take him out and show him how to retrieve the paper again," added Ralph. "Maybe he forgot."

"Perhaps." Mr. Eltison sounded doubtful. "That would be the first time it's ever happened."

Ralph picked up the newspaper, folded it, and then fished a rubber band from the junk drawer. He strapped the newspaper while instructing the new Elt to exit through the doggie door. Once outside, the boy and the dog walked onto the driveway, where Ralph set down the paper. The new Elt sat down beside Ralph and stared at him.

"Okay, every morning you have to do this for my dad," instructed Ralph. "Even if you're not here tomorrow, the next time we have to do this right." Ralph knelt down and awkwardly picked up the paper with his mouth. The task was a little difficult, but he accomplished it. He dropped the paper and stood up, then waved his right hand upwards for Oleo to repeat the action. "Come on," he directed.

Surprisingly, Oleo grabbed the paper with his mouth. Ralph patted the right side of his thigh and motioned for the dog to follow him. Oleo followed Ralph but stopped at the back door and waited for the boy to open it, enter the kitchen, and close the door before he passed through the doggie door. Inside, Ralph pointed to the kitchen chair; his dad's kitchen chair. Oleo understood Ralph's instructions and gently laid the paper down on the chair.

"Good boy!" declared Ralph. He reached into the cabinet and grabbed a dog biscuit. Cautiously, he held the treat under Oleo's nose. The new Elt sniffed the treat, licked it, and then snatched it out of Ralph's hand. He sat down underneath the table and ate his reward. "What do you know?" chuckled Ralph to himself. "He likes the biscuits!"

The rest of the morning found Ralph finishing up a few light chores. Since the new Elt quickly learned how to retrieve the newspaper, Ralph was open to a new challenge. He had trained Elt before. Why not do it again with this Elt? He hoped it wouldn't be too long before his Elt returned, but in the meantime, he figured he'd show the new Elt some of the old Elt's tricks.

First he reviewed 'sit' and 'shake paws.' Without hesitation, the new Elt sat down and shook paws. He then taught Oleo how to roll over by demonstrating it himself on the kitchen floor. Soon Oleo was playing dead on command, too.

Before the transformation, Oleo had reviewed a canine's behavior on board Trianthius I, so he had become familiar with many of a dog's tricks. Ralph was surprised by how easy it was for this new dog to learn these maneuvers, for it had taken Elt much longer to learn them as a puppy. Each time Oleo performed a task, the boy rewarded him with a tasty treat, which made Oleo very pleased.

Next on Ralph's list was the game of catch. He grabbed Elt's favorite red ball and rolled it to Oleo. The new Elt watched the ball roll, and then sniffed it when it came to a complete stop in front of him. Once again Ralph urged the Sorgian to play with the ball and pick it up. Understanding, the new Elt grabbed the ball with his mouth and delivered it to the boy. Ralph rolled the ball down the kitchen floor, a little farther than before. Oleo watched for a second or two, then dashed off, stopped the ball with his nose, nabbed it, and once again brought the ball back to Ralph. Oleo received another treat.

Ralph, used to Elt catching the ball in mid-air, bounced the ball so it crested about four feet in the air. Oleo realized what the human wanted him to do, but the coordination wasn't quite there yet. Oleo leaped, but he was too late. Ralph had to chuckle. Oleo missed the second bounce, too, but he did capture the ball when it stopped rolling, and return it to Ralph. "You really must like these treats," laughed

Ralph. "I only give Elt one treat a day, two if he performs excellently." Ralph reached into the cabinet for one more treat. His "dog" kindly accepted. "Well, I guess you passed the first test. Now let's see if you can fool Jenny and Bernadette."

It was about lunch time and Ralph's dad was just returning from the EATS A LOT Grocery Store. Sometimes Ralph would accompany his dad to the store so he could lobby for some extra snacks. On this day however, Ralph figured he should stay as close to the new Elt as possible.

Stocking all the groceries took less than ten minutes. They were two guys and a dog; and one was ten, and really didn't eat that much. Ralph later fixed sandwiches for his dad and himself while the new Elt lounged under the kitchen table.

Ralph called Jenny to find out if it was okay to come over. Within a few minutes, Ralph was out the door with his dog. Oleo didn't know what was happening, but when Ralph patted his right leg with his right hand, Oleo rose and followed the boy. The dog wasn't sure about the leash, but he let Ralph hook it to his collar. Ralph twisted the green collar, but found no stone attached.

"Now we're going for a walk," said Ralph as they headed down Springhaven Court en route to Jenny's house. "We're going to be walking with Jenny and Bernadette, our friends." Ralph wasn't quite sure if Oleo understood, but it seemed that the replacement dog had responded very well to all of his previous commands. Sure Ralph missed Elt, but he could see that Oleo was trying his best to replicate Elt in every fashion.

When the two reached Jenny's house, Ralph knocked on the side door. He turned around to see if Bryan and Caroline were home, but Professor Greenlee's car was gone and no one was outside playing. Ralph really liked the two new kids, but he preferred to wait until Elt was back to take a walk with them.

Jenny opened the door. "We'll be right there," she smiled. A few minutes later, Jenny returned with Bernadette. "Sorry, just finishing up the dishes."

"That's okay," assured Ralph. "I had some chores today, too."

"Do you want to take an extra long walk today?" asked Jenny. "My mom says we have nowhere to go today."

Ralph always loved his walks with Jenny, Elt, and Bernadette. With Elt being away though, Ralph was a little apprehensive. He didn't want Jenny to detect anything different about Elt. Already, with just a couple of sniffs, Bernadette could definitely sense that Elt wasn't Elt. "Sure, that sounds great," said Ralph nervously. So the four walkers trekked down Valleydale Drive, toward the park on Schoolhouse Road.

Ralph kept the new Elt to his right while Bernadette walked in front of Jenny. Ralph didn't realize it, but he had hastened the pace. He just wanted to get the walk accomplished without any hitches or complications. "I think we're going too fast," said Jenny. "Slow down. We don't have to be back soon."

"Oh, I'm sorry," replied Ralph. "I didn't notice I was going that fast." Ralph slowed down.

Once Bernadette was able to catch her breath, she gazed over at her friend. The new Elt looked straight ahead while he walked. He peered over in Bernadette's direction for a split second but quickly jerked his head back when he met her gaze. Bernadette didn't know what was going on, but she knew something was up. "Is he mad at me?" she wondered.

When they reached the park, the kids stopped at the water fountain. The water wasn't ice cold, but it was wet. The kids splashed some water on themselves and each other, and then flicked some wetness on their pets. Ralph and Jenny drank enough water to just quench their thirst, for they knew that a return to Jenny's house meant a tall glass of fresh lemonade.

After a while, the kids and pets returned to Jenny's house, and once again, Wendy Rodgers set out a big bowl of cold water for Elt and Bernadette. "Let's go in and get some lemonade," said Jenny to Ralph. Ralph was hesitant to leave his dog alone with Bernadette. So far the Cocker Spaniel hadn't barked at the new Elt. It seemed as though Bernadette had not detected anything strange about his temporary companion. Things had gone pretty smoothly and Ralph wanted it to stay that way.

"Sure," Ralph replied uneasily as he released his hold on the new Elt's leash. Jenny opened the door. Ralph followed, glancing back at the two dogs, who were standing by the big water bowl. Bernadette was the first to drink. Ralph closed the door.

When Bernadette finished drinking, she stepped back to allow Elt a chance to approach the bowl. He didn't move. He just sat down right by the porch. "Aren't you thirsty?" asked Bernadette. "It's pretty hot out today."

"I'm okay," replied the new Elt.

Bernadette inched closer to him. She sniffed the air in his direction. Something was not right. It wasn't Elt's normal scent, but there he was, as plain as day. Bernadette didn't know whether to bark, growl, or just stare at her friend. "What's going on?" she finally asked.

The new Elt didn't know how to reply. He continued to look away from her. "I'm fine, I'm okay."

Bernadette couldn't figure it out. The smell wasn't right. Her friend's demeanor was definitely weird. Even his voice didn't sound the same. But it was Elt. Same size, same markings, the same look he had every day. "Are you going to pick me up for the meeting when the darkness falls?" asked Bernadette.

Her friend displayed a puzzled expression. "Pick you up? A meeting?"

"You know, the meeting. We're welcoming the two new pets," stated Bernadette. "You and Jasmine set it up."

"Oh that," returned the new Elt, trying to achieve nonchalance. He fidgeted a moment wondering what to say next.

"Okay, there's something going on with you," declared Bernadette. "You don't smell like Elt. You're definitely acting weirder than ever, and you don't sound like him either! But you look like him. You even have the same collar around your neck."

Evidently, Sorgians kept themselves pretty calm while in their disguises, but Oleo sensed that he wasn't going to pull the wool over Bernadette's eyes. "Okay, okay, I'm not Elt!" he blurted. "My name is Oleo. I'm a replicator."

Bernadette blinked, confused. She didn't know what to think. Was this imposter telling the truth? Where was the real Elt? And why did he look exactly like her friend? "A repli- what?" She shook her head.

"I'm Oleo. I'm from the planet Sorgia."

"What? Well, if you are this dude that looks like my friend, then where is he?" she demanded.

Oleo watched the door. He wanted to make sure that the humans didn't interrupt the explanation he was about to give. He stared up at the sky. "Your friend is up there, somewhere, with Coladeus," replied Oleo.

Bernadette gazed upward, and then back at the new Elt. "Okay, you're telling me that the dude from outer space who talks to Elt stopped by, picked him up, and replaced him with you?" Bernadette's confusion was mixed with disbelief. "How long will he be gone?"

"I don't know," replied Oleo. "Not for long, I hope."

At that point, something in Oleo's body composition went haywire; kind of like when it rains real heavy and knocks out the satellite TV for a few seconds. For just a flash of a second or two, Bernadette witnessed what the being beside her really was. A sense of horror and awe overcame her. Then, as fast as it occurred, Elt's form was back again, like nothing had ever happened.

"Well, I believe you, but it's really weird," breathed Bernadette. Both of them heard the children at the screen door. "Remember, meet me here at dark, after your humans are asleep," she whispered. Oleo nodded. The screen door opened. Ralph and Jenny returned to their dogs.

"What are you doing tomorrow?" asked Ralph.

"Ah, I don't know," returned Jenny.

"Wanna go swimming?" asked Ralph.

"That sounds like fun," said Jenny. 'I'll ask my mom and call you later."

"Bye," said Ralph.

Jenny waved bye as she grabbed Bernadette's leash and led her Cocker Spaniel inside. Bernadette watched Ralph and his dog walk away. She wondered if Ralph knew that the Elt he was walking really wasn't Elt. When would her friend return? What was he doing up there in space with Coladeus?

Bernadette knew that there was some kind of alien presence involved with Elt's super powers. Elt had proven that fact when he communicated with Coladeus at the warehouse a couple of months before. She had heard someone speak to him on the transmitter. What could be going on? Why did Coladeus need Elt's help? Were there more bad humans? Bernadette's mind was full of questions, but there was no one there to answer them.

Bernadette drank some more water and nibbled on the left over dry dog food that was given to her earlier in the day. While Jenny sat down to read a book, Bernadette rested on her doggie bed. There was something strange going on with her. The last time she worried about Elt, she was right there in the same place with him, trapped in cages at the old warehouse. She knew that they were in deep trouble, but at least she knew where he was. The thought of her friend up there in space, possibly in danger, made Bernadette uneasy.

She hoped he would come home soon. Maybe Elt would return before the neighborhood pet meeting. How would she be able to convince the other pets that the imposter was Elt? They would surely figure it out eventually from his odd scent and very strange behavior. Bernadette thought deeply for the rest of the day and into the evening. Maybe she could make the excuse that Elt wasn't feeling well. She would do all the talking. Maybe it would work. That was her plan. She soon napped by her human.

Ralph walked his dog home thinking that they had pulled off the whole Elt replacement thing. Well, at least Jenny didn't figure it out. Ralph didn't know what Jenny's dog knew, but he breathed a huge sigh of relief. He hoped he could go swimming the next day. The dogs weren't allowed at the pool, a clever ploy by Ralph to keep "his dog" hidden from Jenny and Bernadette. Ralph, like Bernadette, hoped that Elt would return soon. Although he kind of had fun with Oleo, he really missed his Elt.

Ralph and Oleo stayed home for the rest of the day into the night. All the activities, and staying up the night before were definite fatigue factors. Oleo slept under the dining room table while Ralph helped his dad with the dishes after dinner. Ralph then bathed and went to bed. The day had been an exhausting one. His dog remained asleep under the table for most of the night, but at some point, the new Elt woke up and crawled into bed beside the boy. Oleo too thought about how long it would take Elt to return. Coladeus had told him one or two Earth days if the mission was a success. He had tried his best, but Elt's best friend had figured him out.

Many, many miles away in space, Elt's mission had already begun.

CHAPTER 7

ELT SCANNED THE ROOM BEFORE him. Only one creature before him resembled anyone from Earth. He was excited, but a bit apprehensive. Elt really wasn't an outgoing canine. He loved his humans and he was familiar with the neighborhood pets, but that was enough for him.

"I introduce Elt from Earth," announced Matheun. With that, a canine, a Golden Retriever to be exact, approached Elt, and raised his right paw.

"Paw bump dude. Welcome to the team," grinned the canine. A bit surprised, Elt raised his right paw to receive the paw bump, which resembled the human version of fist bumping, but with paws. "I'm Sparky," he continued. "I'm sure Coladeus has told you all about me." Elt stood silent, thinking, and then shook his head no. "Really?" asked Sparky in disbelief. "You know, Sparky from California; the Righteous Retriever...saved the Golden State from becoming an island..."

Elt apologetically shook his head again. Sparky, deciding to change the subject, shook himself, as if he was shaking off water from a bath or rainstorm. "Phew, it gets cold in this spaceship. I'm used to the hot summery weather in San Francisco. I heard about you, though. You and your crew caught some really bodacious bad guys." Sparky swaggered away from Elt. "But, you let the head dude get away."

Elt suddenly found his voice. "But he left in a big human flying machine. What was I supposed to do?"

Sparky rolled his eyes. "Fly, of course."

"What? In front of humans? I couldn't do that." Elt didn't want Sparky to know that he hadn't mastered the art of flying yet. Sparky just chuckled and led Elt to another teammate seated at the briefing room table.

"This is Klecktonis, from the planet… I can't remember," announced Sparky unapologetically. Klecktonis was an odd-looking creature. Sparky wasn't quite sure if Klecktonis was male or female, or if the planet it originated from even had males and females. Grayish and brown in color, the being possessed a very large head, pointed on three sides. One would have thought with that head, Klecktonis would have been a perfect Trianthian. The being nodded to Elt. "Don't make her mad," added Sparky under his breath. "She can zap you with her eyes." Elt watched Klecktonis carefully as he passed by, still following the Golden Retriever.

"Next is my brother Myotaur," Sparky said. "He's really not my brother." Myotaur resembled a giant blue Hercules, but with horns that pointed to the sky. His overall height was way over six feet. "I thought I was strong, but this guy," stated Sparky. "Let's just say the stone gives him super amazing strength and abilities. Don't try to paw wrestle him."

"Do they understand what you're saying to me?" asked Elt.

Sparky stopped and chuckled. "Not a word. But Coladeus says we'll form a great team." The two stopped before the last member of the team. The creature was black and gray and resembled a spider, but only had six legs. "And this is Widenmauer," announced Sparky. "He, uh, likes to use his legs; let's just keep it at that."

Widenmauer extended one of his legs across the table, and gestured for Elt to shake his claw. Elt responded by leaping onto the table and respectfully shaking with his right paw.

"Time to take our seats," said Sparky. "The boss is about to brief us."

Elt asked quickly, "Is this your first mission outside of Calif… Calif…?"

"California," finished Sparky. "And no, I've journeyed with Coladeus on many missions in my short life. This is the first one in a long time though. It must be something special."

"Do you have one of those things… those beings that replace you while you're gone?" inquired Elt.

"A Sorgian? Yep," replied Sparky. "My human doesn't even know I'm gone. My replicator does a righteously good job. Before you know it, I'm home and everything is good."

The lights in the room began to dim. Then they proceeded to brighten. Dim...brighten...dim. The lights finally brightened one last time. Matheun, who had been reading through a scanner while Elt was being introduced, glanced up to address the team. "Coladeus approaches."

The briefing room door opened with a quiet hum and Coladeus made a quick entrance, his body gliding smoothly across the floor. He stepped up to the podium. The lights remained on.

In front of each teammate there were razor-thin, curved computer tablets, similar to but more complex than the computer screens on Earth. Each screen demonstrated different sound and word patterns, so each crewmember understood in their native language what the computer was transmitting. Each computer screen flashed and beeped, but the beeping and flashing stopped momentarily as Coladeus prepared to speak.

On top of the podium rested an eight inch black device. It was a portable distranslator, but this one was more sophisticated than others Elt had seen. It deciphered Coladeus' words and then sent the message to each individual computer screen, in the dialect that each individual would understand.

"Thank you for your participation," Coladeus began. "The mission in which we are about to partake is simple, yet crucial to one civilization's very existence." With the help of a tiny microphone attached to a small necklace around his neck, Coladeus was free to mingle around the room while he spoke. Elt noticed that he couldn't hear the Trianthian directly. Coladeus's voice transmitted from the computer screen in front of him, in perfect canine speak. Elt gazed around the room. His other teammates, including Sparky, watched their computer screens intently.

It was time to get serious. He was about to discover the "wheres" and "whys" of the mission.

Elt scanned his screen. A picture of a planet appeared. Elt had no idea what a planet was, let alone which planet was pictured on his screen. The planet was round, with multitudes of multi-colored rings encircling it. "The planet on your screen is referred to as Saturn," continued Coladeus. "Surrounding Saturn are nine satellites or 'moons' as they are named."

Elt and Sparky watched their screens as the picture zoomed in, featuring the colorful rings and the various revolving moons. The projection zoomed in even further, focusing on the largest moon. "This moon is named 'Titan,'" reported Coladeus. The image continued moving closer and closer to the largest moon, until it revealed a computer animated view of the surface. "Titan's properties enable life," explained Coladeus, "although life can be challenging, considering the conditions that exist on the moon's surface."

Coladeus stepped over to the podium once again where Matheun joined him and took over the narrative. "Six duraceps ago, members of our Trianthian crew, led by Coladeus, assisted a group of citizens from the planet Tsar. Their mission: to colonize a particular region of Titan. The Tsarians had put together a well-designed settlement at the foot of a mountainous range with a sustainable supply of water." Matheun continued to speak. "From time to time, crews from both Trianthius I and Trianthius II have visited the colonists on Titan. They have reported no serious issues. Their health has been satisfactory. The atmospheric conditions, although challenging, haven't worsened."

Coladeus picked up the explanation. "During our recent travels to Earth and Venus, we received transmissions from the Tsarians describing difficulties with one of their sustaining stations. It appears that the cause of the malfunction was due to the elements. However, we have not ruled out the possibility of outside interference." Pictures of the sustaining station compound, resembling a mini power plant, appeared on the computer screens. The compound housed the Tsarian living quarters, along with their water, power, and waste treatment plants.

A close up of a pipeline, part of the water purifying system, popped up on the screen. From a nearby ravine, the purifying pipeline pumped in water which was actually poisonous for consumption. The pipeline brought the water into the treatment plant for cleaning and processing so it could be used as a valuable resource by the colonists. The picture zoomed in on a sizeable crack that had formed on the main pipeline. The pipe system rose about thirty feet high before it connected to a fitting that led to the inside of the treatment plant.

"As you can see," stated Matheun, "the main pipeline is in danger of erupting. If it does erupt, life for the Tsarians on Titan will be greatly threatened, for they will have no fresh water. The Tsarians already lost many lives while building that facility, due to the harsh conditions. We do not want to see that colony compromised." The screen once again flashed to the picture of Titan. "Our mission," concluded Coladeus, "is to travel to Titan and repair the pipeline before it erupts."

Klecktonis gazed up at Coladeus and gave "her" nod of approval. Myotaur was next, then Widenmauer. Finally, Elt and Sparky nodded their heads, too. "We are en route to Saturn as we speak," stated Coladeus. "We shall be there shortly. If any of your stones require recharging, go to the re-energizing chamber now, please. Our quarters are small, so this is where our guests usually rest. We ask that the team remain here until further notice. Refreshments will be served shortly."

Sparky raised his right paw. "I have a question please."

"Yes Sparky," replied Coladeus.

"Us Earth creatures, we need a place, you know...to take care of business. Usually outside, you know," hinted Sparky. "Do you, uh, have such a place?" Sparky shot a quick glance at Elt, widened his eyes, and then turned his attention back to the Trianthian leader.

"We will provide such a place for you," answered a smiling Coladeus.

"Phew," uttered Sparky. "Man, I've needed to go since we picked you up, Elt."

"When it is time to beam down to Titan's surface, we will notify you," announced Coladeus with an air of finality as he and Matheun strode towards the exit.

"Uh, wait, beam down?" Elt squinted in confusion.

Coladeus paused near the door. "Something new we're trying," he admitted. The door in the briefing room hummed opened. Matheun and Coladeus stepped out, and the door closed behind them.

"What is that supposed to mean?" asked Elt. "What does 'beaming down' mean?"

Sparky got up and paced around the desk to face Elt. "Not sure, but I'm sure we'll be just fine. Their little space pod thing only seats two, so they had to do something to get us all down faster."

The door hummed again. A Trianthian crew member, younger and a little smaller than Matheun, entered. Scanning the team members, he spotted Sparky, motioned for the retriever to follow, and quickly turned away. Sparky dashed toward the Trianthian in a flash, and soon he too was out of the briefing room.

Until this moment, Elt had followed Sparky's movements. Now he felt alone and uncertain in the room with the others, especially Klecktonis. Elt's eyes suddenly shifted to the alien. His eyes met her eyes. Her eyes began to glow. With a gasp, the super dog quickly diverted his attention, remembering Sparky's warning. Whew. While he exhaled and blinked, he realized he had seen her green gem on a necklace around her neck. Evidently, Klecktonis had no concerns about concealing her stone from anyone on her planet, or whatever world she originated from.

Myotaur rose and drifted over to the entrance, pulling his stone out from a pouch on his belt to inspect it. The giant's humongous torso seemed to possess muscles on top of muscles. Elt felt small and wondered why this being needed any form of extra strength.

Widenmauer remained in his seat, his six legs folded to conceal how long they really were. He appeared to be resting, but Elt only glanced over his way for a second or two. The short glance was enough to notice the stone embedded in his skin around his neck.

Moments later, Sparky returned, and Myotaur left with the young Trianthian usher. Sparky jumped back on his seat with his reassuring confidence and energy. "Dude, I'm really hungry. I hope they serve cheeseburgers. But I doubt it." Now Elt had tasted the turkey and stuffing from Thanksgiving, but had never tasted one of Ralph's cheeseburgers. "Cheeseburgers are the best human food in the world," bragged Sparky.

"Where did you just go?" asked Elt.

"They led me to a small area like a small piece of my yard. It did the trick."

"Did you see anything? Like the beamer thing?" asked Elt. "I wonder how long the mission will be. I hope my human isn't missing me too much."

"Your human will be fine," soothed Sparky. "At least he knows you're gone. My humans think I'm still in San Francisco."

Two Trianthians entered then, leading a rolling cart; it didn't roll on wheels, so it was more like a floating cart. There were several styles of refreshments on the cart, some of which looked very strange to Elt and Sparky. The Trianthians stopped in front of Klecktonis first. One of them reached for a long glass filled with some kind of green juice and two long straws. On the surface of the liquid, a slight haze of steam brewed. Elt couldn't tell if the liquid was hot or cold. Klecktonis accepted the drink and sipped it immediately with one of the straws.

Widenmauer arose out of his sleep when he heard the crewmembers enter. His legs began to extend outward and his head rose when he noticed his meal on the cart. All wrapped inside a clear box, there appeared to be a giant bug-like creature, maybe a giant beetle, black, with a touch of red and white on its back.

Elt and Sparky watched the spider-like creature accept his meal. With two of his legs, he opened the box and let the beetle crawl out. Then they watched a horrifying sight. Widenmauer leaped upon his prey and began to spin and wrap it in a web-like substance. Within seconds, the beetle was totally encased. The dogs had to look away when in the next moment, the alien's fangs pierced and drank the life out of the bug. "Gross, gnarley dude," grimaced Sparky to Elt. "I am not messing with him either."

Myotaur came back into the briefing room, placing his newly re-energized stone back into his belt pouch. The Trianthian crewmembers handed the giant blue marvel a green glass containing multi-colored sticks; maybe eight or nine of them. Myotaur immediately shook out a stick and began to chew on it.

"It's the closest food to human so far," remarked Elt. Sparky agreed.

Now it was time for the two canines to see what the Trianthians had prepared for them. The crew mates moved the cart closer to the dogs and then served each one of them a silver covered dish.

"Thank you," Elt attempted but he noticed that neither crewmember wore a distransulator, so communication was impossible.

"Do you want to open it up first?" asked Sparky.

"Together," replied Elt.

Sparky nodded in agreement. They both removed the covers with their right paws. "I don't believe it. How did they know?"

Elt sniffed the meal. "It smells like it." He then took a taste and looked sideways at Sparky. "Tastes like it too." Elt stopped talking and got busy eating.

Sparky gazed at his dish. "Well, it's not cheeseburgers, but it sure looks tasty. I'm hungrier than a grizzly bear in a salmon stream." Sparky dug in and quickly devoured his meal of delicious moist dog food.

Once the refreshments were finished and the team was satisfied, the crewmembers returned and collected their dishes. As if on cue, the computer screens flashed and Matheun's image appeared. "It is time to prepare for the mission. Please pay attention to your individual screen, for each screen will dictate your assignment. We will send you to the transport area soon."

Matheun's image on Elt's screen faded. A diagram of the cracked pipeline appeared. Elt scrutinized the computer-generated image of himself holding a rope that was tied around the pipeline. His role in the mission was to work together with Myotaur, to steady and straighten the pipeline while the other teammates worked on repairing the crack.

Studying his own screen, Sparky discovered that his role was to fly the rope around the pipeline, secure it, and then deliver it to Elt. He would then assist Elt and Myotaur if needed.

"Do you understand your roles for the mission?" asked Matheun. "Press the X on your touch screen if you do." Every mission teammate touched their screens simultaneously. "Excellent," responded Matheun. "We will now prepare you for the trip to the surface of Titan. Please follow the crewmember."

Precisely timed, the humming of the door ushered in a Trianthian. No one could really tell if it was the same Trianthian that entered every time. Klecktonis rose, Myotaur, Widenmauer, and the two canines followed. They trailed the glowing light of the Trianthian out of the briefing room and down a long, dark hallway. The penetrating light of Klecktonis's eyes, also lit the way. "I hope she doesn't have those eyes on full power," murmured Sparky. "She'll tear a hole in this ship with those eyes."

The group stopped at an elevator and the Trianthian directed them inside. It was a little tight, especially with Widenmauer's long legs, but they all squeezed in. The elevator door whisked closed, and they descended to the third level.

Elt and Sparky were the first two out with the others right behind. A new Trianthian crewmember ushered them hastily through a short hall and into another room where Coladeus was already waiting for their arrival. The Trianthian leader was equipped with a small mask and air tank, his normal distransulator looped around his neck. He adjusted the device and spoke to Klecktonis first, then Myotaur, Widenmauer, and finally, Elt and Sparky.

"The surface on Titan can be unstable" warned Coladeus. "We will equip you with a mask and a small air tank belt. In addition, you will have to battle the lack of gravity. On board Trianthius I, we simulate gravity, but down there, you will have to maintain a steady stride, or you will be flying."

"Did you say flying?" asked Elt.

"Not that kind of flying," replied Coladeus. "The loss of gravity will make it seem like everyone is flying."

Trianthian crewmembers handed out air tank equipment to each mission crew member. Sparky and Elt would need oxygen when they reached the planet's surface. Trianthius I used oxygen in its life support system, but the other creatures on board needed elements infused into their tanks that would help them sustain their needs.

Once they received their equipment, the mission crew followed Coladeus to a platform that contained four tube-like modules; two large and two small. The larger modules could support a larger being like Myotaur or Widenmauer. The smaller ones would benefit Klecktonis, Sparky, or Elt.

Coladeus once again spoke into his distransulator. "We have been experimenting with a new system of transportation. The pod has been a very successful method, but it does take a long time and could be detected too easily, especially with the improvement of many of the planetary satellite systems that we are encountering now. This new technique will speed us to our destination instantaneously." Coladeus pointed to the modules. "These modules, designed with our advanced technology and fueled by our Trianthian stones, will send your body to its destination, safe and intact."

Klecktonis raised her hand and asked a question. Coladeus answered. He spoke in turn to the other two aliens, and then addressed Elt and Sparky. "Klecktonis wanted to know if we have tested the modules before. I informed her that we have been testing the procedure for about one duracep, but only with Trianthians and Sorgians. This will be the first time that we transport members of your species, but we feel quite confident that the modules will be successful. I will be traveling with you to make sure that we all make it to Titan's surface successfully."

Sparky and Elt didn't fully understand what they were about to encounter, but they knew that if they stepped into those tube-like things, somehow they would end up on Titan. They were definitely putting their trust in Coladeus.

A screen opened in front of them revealing the planet Saturn. Matheun then swept into the room. "We are approaching the planet," announced the first officer. "We shall be in the range of Titan shortly."

The mission team watched the screen closely. Although it seemed like a relatively simple mission, it would be dangerous, and a first for Elt. His original mission had been a challenging one, but it was on Earth, his home planet, and in his hometown. What would Titan be like? The transportation vehicle...would it work? Many questions filled Elt's mind as he checked his equipment. He was about to embark on a new and exciting adventure, but his excitement was laced with apprehension.

CHAPTER 8

PROFESSOR ANNOUNCES LAUNCH DATE OF TIME MACHINE shouted the headline from the Herald newspaper on the very morning that Oleo didn't fetch the paper for Mr. Eltison. Ralph's dad later opened the paper to discover the monumental news of the day, the most significant news of the century!

The announcement of an operational time machine not only rocked Spring Valley, but through the media of the internet, television, newspaper, and radio, the message rocketed around the globe. Representatives from almost every country in the world would travel to Spring Valley for the historic launch.

The actual ceremony would take place inside the small laboratory where the time machine would launch. The lab was barely big enough to hold Van Hausen, Greenlee, Livingstone, and the time machine with its costly, delicate equipment. But somehow they would allow for a limited number of press, staff, and family members to attend.

The public was welcome to assemble on the campus green between the buildings. A stage would be erected outside the facility where thousands of folks could watch the event on huge screens. For folks that wanted to stay home, there would be live coverage on every major television network.

Between the hot summer day when he spoke in the auditorium, and the eve of the launch, Professor Van Hausen conducted two more test runs to insure the safety of the travelers. He also wanted to really make sure the time machine worked. During those tests, Professor Greenlee monitored all the functioning parts of the machine, Edward checked the vitals on the display console, and Van Hausen, once again acted as the time traveler.

On the first trip he traveled into the future. Since he enjoyed space travel, Van Hausen voyaged one hundred years into the future, and set his destination for Cape Canaveral, Florida, the site where NASA's rockets and space shuttles had soared into space for the last fifty years. Set to return only fifteen minutes later, the professor spent an equivalent of one Earth day at Cape Canaveral. Upon his return, Van Hausen was excited, yet quiet about the whole adventure.

"What did you see?" insisted Edward.

"What was the status of America's space program?" pleaded Stanley.

"Very interesting," was the only comment Van Hausen uttered. He didn't want to say much about what he saw, for he wanted to make sure that he didn't alter the future with any of his actions or words. Stanley and Edward recognized Van Hausen's trip as a success. The professor alluded to only one glitch; his landing location was slightly off course. Fortunately, no one saw him, so he remained anonymous. "We will need to fine tune the directional coordinate controls," Van Hausen advised his team.

On the second experimental trip, Van Hausen wanted to travel into the past, but much further back in time than on his first trip, and definitely not within Spring Valley or any of its outlying areas. Going back thirty years was simple enough and remarkable. But if he could travel back...way back...like to the time of the Egyptians building the pyramids, or when dinosaurs roamed the Earth, now that would be amazing! As the day of that test trip approached, Van Hausen knew that he had to make a decision. He finally settled on the time period that had always enthralled him when he was a kid, the time period he had always wanted to live in. He chose the Roman Empire, circa 44 B.C.

Professor Van Hausen, along with his two associates, calculated the formulas that would blast him to the deep past. The trip to the Roman Empire would not require the machine's maximum output of energy, but the calculations would have to be exact. It was going to be risky, and the professor knew it, but he wanted to make sure that this marvel of his really worked before he allowed others to travel in it.

"This magnificent wonder we have created will make our observatory famous!" exalted the professor. "To say nothing about making millions and millions of dollars!" he laughed incredulously. The professor really wasn't in it for the money, but he was keenly aware of the large number of bills needing to be paid, and his observatory needed new computers and equipment. Surely there would be many people around the world that would pay top dollar to venture through time in his time machine.

But what about the future? Van Hausen knew that travelers to the future as well as the past wouldn't be able to interfere with any event, or he or she might alter world history. The full ramifications and possible consequences of time travel swirled in Van Hausen's mind, and in the mind of his partner, Professor Stanley Greenlee.

Back in the laboratory, Edward could clearly see what was happening. Although he had been a faithful and trustworthy associate of Van Hausen's, Professor Greenlee had snaked between them and diminished Edward's value to Van Hausen. It wasn't fair. "Professor, may I please have the honor of accompanying you on this voyage to the Roman Empire?" pleaded Edward, trying not to sound angry or desperate.

The professor shook his head. "I'm so sorry Edward, but I feel you should assist Professor Greenlee, so we can make sure I make it back home." Edward nodded politely and agreed, but inside he was seething.

A week later, the last trial run commenced. The professor was seated alone in the time machine, with Professor Greenlee and Edward standing by the console, clipboards and stop watches in their hands. Professor Greenlee noticed a brown box resembling a satchel, strapped to the floor under the professor's seat. "What do you have in the bag?" he asked.

"Oh, just a few things one might need in 44 B.C.," smiled Professor Van Hausen. "You know, a toga, sandals, a few scrolls. But don't worry, I will keep concealed my compass, binoculars, and watch, of course."

"Smart thinking," agreed Professor Greenlee.

Edward scanned the coordinates on a computer screen that was located on the console. "I've isolated an area just outside Rome, like you requested."

"Good," chuckled Van Hausen. "We don't want the time machine to land right in the middle of the Coliseum, do we?"

"We've studied the geographical maps of that period all week," stated professor Greenlee. "If history is correct, and the information on population density is accurate, we should land you in a remote location, safe for landing and safe for launching back home."

"Excellent!" Van Hausen's smile was endless.

Professor Greenlee and Edward Livingstone pressed several buttons and switches to initiate the launch. The hum of the machine began low and then slowly rose to pre-launch pitch. Edward paused for a few seconds, and then gave the professor a nod. Van Hausen secured his oxygen mask and gave a "thumbs up." "Gentlemen, I will see you in thirty minutes," he cried out over the roar.

"It's more like a tad over two thousand years, Professor," hollered Greenlee.

The platform began to spin as Greenlee and Edward continued to operate the controls. Smoke from the friction on the platform began to emanate from the bottom, causing thin fog to spread around the room. The time machine spun faster, faster, faster, until it blurred into its required top speed. Professor Greenlee triggered the final application.

BAM! The mini-explosion occurred, causing flashing, searing light and producing thicker smoke. When it finally cleared, about fifteen seconds later, the time machine was gone. Stanley grinned and shared a victorious look with Edward. Then they both proceeded to the platform, which was still spinning, but slowing down. Once the platform came to a complete stop, Stanley wrote down a few notes on his clipboard, checked his watch, and then jotted down the time. Edward walked back over to the console and began monitoring the settings, hoping for a successful return in thirty minutes.

"I do believe the professor is on his way to the Roman Empire!" affirmed Stanley. "I hope all is well." Edward nodded in reply. For the time being, it was his responsibility to help Greenlee return Professor

Van Hausen safely, along with the time machine, of course. Edward remained friendly and professional.

Professor Van Hausen strained to keep his eyes open during the journey, but the force was so overwhelming, he could barely see a thing. This trip to the past was different from the first one. The professor figured he had far more time-distance to cover, for the first trip was only back to 1975. His new destination was countless generations before that.

As the trip continued, Van Hausen floated away through space. Was it space or was it time he was traveling through? The blur to his right resembled Earth, and his time machine reversed at incredible speeds around the planet. Nearing the destination, Van Hausen's machine began to slow down and drift through the clouds. He soared effortlessly over some mountain ranges until he came to rest on a piece of flat terrain.

The professor pulled off his mask and unfastened his seat belt. Where was he? Was he in Rome? He reached into his satchel and retrieved the clothes he had packed. He quickly changed into his toga and sandals. Adjusting his watch, which was still miraculously functioning despite all the force inflicted on it through the trip, Van Hausen noticed that the minute hand didn't move every minute. The quantum module facilitator was synched to his watch. One minute of "time machine time" wasn't the same as normal time.

The professor knew if he kept a close eye on his watch, he would be okay. It wouldn't operate like a normal watch. He was given about twelve hours to investigate the past, but when he returned to present day, only a half hour would have transpired. He knew he would have to keep his watch hidden, for a timepiece of the future should not be noticed by the people from the past. Van Hausen was now ready to venture out.

The machine's door hissed open and the professor stepped out into fresh air. He pulled a compass from his pocket and realized he needed to veer west. Some brush nearby concealed the time machine fairly well. He didn't want to travel too far, for if he was discovered, chances of returning to the time machine would be slim.

Van Hausen headed uphill in hopes of finding some hint of civilization at the top. During the climb, he discovered what appeared to be a dirt road that ran all the way up the mountain. Following the quiet road for some time, the professor gradually registered a noise that seemed to be heading his way. The noise drew nearer.

Quickly, Van Hausen rushed over and hid behind a huge boulder situated about twenty feet from the dirt road. The approaching noise turned out to be a couple of sentries on their horses. Van Hausen peeked cautiously, for he definitely wanted to see without being seen. Unaware of the peeping stranger, the sentries dutifully plodded past Van Hausen, speaking to each other in Latin as they went on by.

When he believed it was safe, Van Hausen emerged from behind the rock and continued his trek up the road, in the same direction as the sentries. Finally reaching the top of the hill, he stopped for a moment to scan the scene before him. If there was any doubt that the professor had traveled to the correct time period, it was quickly erased, for what the professor witnessed was truly Caesar's Rome.

With the use of his binoculars, the professor spotted the Roman Coliseum way off in the distance. It was magnificent. He could hear a crowd roaring from the structure, even this far away. Were there gladiators in the Coliseum? "What was I thinking? Rome is way too big to visit in such a short time." He exhaled in disappointment, then shook it off and got down to business.

"Based on the angle I'm facing, I should be walking down Esquiline Hill," thought the professor. Esquiline Hill was one of the seven hills that outlined Rome. Van Hausen started to trek downhill. His goal for such a short time was to mingle with the Roman citizens, but not too much. "Wouldn't it be great to see Julius Caesar or any of the Roman Senators?" Van Hausen dreamed.

The professor soon became very uncomfortable, for even though he was clothed in appropriate Roman attire, he still felt out of place. "What if I get caught?" he thought. Then he realized, "Get caught doing what?"

He made it to the bottom of the hill and quietly mingled with the unsuspecting Romans. He spoke to no one; he just observed, but before he knew it, a good part of the day had passed, and Van Hausen recognized that he needed to make his way back over the hill to return to the time machine. For much of his life, all of his thoughts and efforts had been spent on getting to a place like Rome, but not much on what to do when he got there. The whole subject of interfering with both past and future time would need to be discussed again with Edward and Stanley before the next trip.

The professor returned to the time machine, relieved that it was still intact and hidden. After he removed the brushy camouflage, the professor strapped himself in and checked his watch. Twenty-eight present-time minutes had passed, so he had made it back in time. He just hoped that no one would pass by while he waited to be transported back to his time.

Before he knew it, the machine began to hum and spin and in short order, Van Hausen was back in his laboratory, the time machine resting on the rotating platform. When the smoke cleared, Van Hausen unstrapped his belt and took off his mask. He attempted to stand up, but his legs were weak from the trip, so he collapsed back into his seat.

"Whoa Professor," Stanley warned as he hurried over to assist his partner. "You've had quite the trip. Just sit for a few minutes and allow those legs to adjust."

Edward followed Stanley. Although he smiled, the anger inside was still burning. Oh how he had wanted to share the ride to Rome with Professor Van Hausen! "How was the Roman Empire?" Edward asked with forced enthusiasm.

The professor paused for a few seconds taking a couple of deep breaths. "It was vast. Enormous," answered Van Hausen, shaking his head. "I should have chosen a smaller place to visit."

Stanley chuckled as he bent over to check Van Hausen's pulse. "What did you see?" he asked.

"I saw it all in front of me," answered Van Hausen. "I believe I was on Esquiline Hill, but even with my compass it was hard to tell."

"Fascinating," grinned Stanley.

"Two sentries passed by me," continued Van Hausen. "I also mingled with the commoners a bit. I completely fit in with the citizens of 44 B.C., although I started to feel anxious for a while. I would have loved to have seen Caesar, but that would have been too risky."

"Let's try standing up again," offered Stanley.

Van Hausen stood, and this time his legs didn't fail him. He stepped out of the time machine, walked straight to the console, and scanned the readings on the screens. "Was it difficult bringing me back?" he wondered.

"A little tricky," admitted Greenlee.

"It was hard to tell on my end," related Van Hausen. "You have to feel the rush when you travel. It is absolutely indescribable."

"I'm sure I will one day," returned Greenlee.

"Absolutely, won't we all," added Edward, wryly.

Van Hausen smiled. "I am famished. I wasn't sure if I should eat before traveling, but I could sure eat a burger from Brown's right about now. Would you two care to join me?"

"Absolutely," exclaimed a smiling Stanley.

"Ah, Professor," spoke Edward with feigned regret, "I'm afraid I have some important errands to run. Forgive me if I do not join you and Professor Greenlee for dinner."

"That is quite alright," assured Van Hausen. "We'll catch up with you tomorrow, bright and early."

So Edward left, and Van Hausen changed back into his regular attire. The two professors drove to town for a bite to eat, or in the hungry Van Hausen's case, a meal to eat.

At Brown's Restaurant, when Stanley was about to bite into his sandwich, Van Hausen told him the exciting news. "Stanley, I want you to travel twenty-five years into the future."

Greenlee bit down in shock, chewed, and then swallowed. "Well, I guess we can plan that for our next test trip."

"No, there will be no more test trips," announced Van Hausen. "The next trip, the one to twenty-five years into the future, will be witnessed by the whole world. You will take off in the time machine and return--on camera!"

"You mean you want me to travel into the future for the big one, the main event?" asked Greenlee.

"Precisely," returned Van Hausen. "And, I want the time machine to be full, all four seats filled. We can hold a contest to fill the seats or something."

Professor Greenlee took a couple of deep breaths. "Wow Professor, I'd be honored, but the time machine is your baby, your lifelong dream."

"But you made it happen," Van Hausen said firmly. "Without you, I'd probably be working on another failed experiment. You deserve this."

"Does Edward know about this?" inquired Greenlee. "He's been a big part of the time machine research, too."

"He knows. I told him this morning," returned Van Hausen. "He understands."

"Well, if that's the case, and you want me on board," stated Greenlee, "then I will travel with my family. We are four in total."

"Then the four of you will travel to the future!" declared Van Hausen.

So it was decided. Professor Greenlee and his family were going to travel to the future and check out Spring Valley in twenty-five years. The decision had to clear one obstacle, however,...Mrs. Greenlee. If it was okay with Mom, then the Greenlee family would be the first family to travel through time. In less than two weeks, Spring Valley would be recognized worldwide. The date was set. The travelers were chosen, and so was the destination.

What wasn't known was that someone else had different plans for the time machine. While the two professors celebrated at Brown's, someone was very busy working late in the laboratory. He possessed a key, and identification, for he had worked at the observatory for many years.

Edward Livingstone jotted some figures down on his clipboard. Then he removed the computer chip that Greenlee had designed and inserted a new chip in its place. "You think you're going to be the first one traveling, Greenlee," sneered Edward. "But, I have other plans for your trip, and plans for a couple of trips of my own."

Edward turned off all the lights in the laboratory. He would return the next morning to meet with the two professors for the planning of the main event. He would also return the next evening to keep working on his own plan once the professors had left. A trip into the future was planned, and everyone thought it was going to be exciting. What Edward had planned for the time machine and the future of Spring Valley wasn't so pleasant at all.

CHAPTER 9

Oleo had slept most of the day and part of the night. He wasn't quite sure of the exact time that Bernadette wanted to meet him, so he decided to slowly crawl out of bed. He exited the kitchen through the doggie door. It was going to be difficult for Oleo to jump over the fence, for he surely didn't possess Elt's super powers. After a couple of failed attempts, the new Elt leaped, balanced, and finally willed himself over the fence. In just a few minutes, he stood in front of Bernadette's house. The Cocker Spaniel and the tabby were seated just outside their yards.

"Were you waiting long?" inquired the new Elt.

"Not really," Bernadette replied.

"But what took you so long, anyway?" complained Jasmine, a bit irritated.

"I had trouble leaping over my fence," replied Oleo, honestly.

"Ha. That's a funny one," retorted Jasmine as they made their way over to the Greenlee's house. The two dogs and feline waited just outside the Greenlee's gate, just far enough back to stay out of sight.

Within a few minutes, the Greenlee's outside light snapped on, Mrs. Greenlee opened the door, and out walked Seymour and Trixie.

The dog and cat ambled down the steps, took care of their business, and tip-toed cautiously towards the gate. From the other side of the fence, Jasmine, Bernadette, and the new Elt appeared.

"Are you ready?" whispered Jasmine.

"Sure," giggled Trixie. "But how do we get out of here?"

Seymour leaped easily over the top of the fence. "You mean how do *you* get out of here?" Seymour plopped down to the ground by the other pets.

Bernadette walked over to the front gate latch. Elt had shown her how to open her own front gate, but this latch wasn't as easy. "Let Elt do it," offered Jasmine.

"Not sure if he can help me on this one," returned Bernadette.

Oleo did manage to assist Bernadette by allowing her to jump on his back. From that vantage point, she was able to work more efficiently on the latch. Within a couple of minutes, Bernadette had it open.

"Thank you ever so much," sang Trixie as she pranced out of her yard. Bernadette nudged the gate almost closed, allowing just enough room for Trixie to return safely.

When the group entered Juan's garage, Sarge was nibbling on one of the Chihuahua's tasty biscuits. Juan was there to greet Trixie and Seymour, while Chin was sitting in the back corner, his eyes closed. Prince and Max hadn't arrived yet.

Sarge gulped down the last morsel. With awe, he noticed the stunningly beautiful Trixie before him. Just like Elt, the Boxer couldn't keep his eyes off of her. Trixie minced up to the Boxer with Seymour following closely behind.

"How do ya do ma'am?" Sarge proclaimed. "My name is Sarge. I'm what you call the leader of our establishment."

"And I'm Juan," interjected the excited Chihuahua.

"Oh no, not this again," thought Bernadette, shaking her head.

"My lands, you fellas are so polite around here," murmured Trixie coyly.

"Much obliged," beamed Sarge. Reluctantly he tore his attention away from the poodle to gaze very quickly around the room, and then settled his sights back on her. "We'll give those two just a few more minutes. The meeting has to be quick."

Seymour then pushed in front of Trixie to be noticed by Sarge. "Hello Old Boy, I'm Seymour Greenlee, one of the London Greenlees, third generation that is." Seymour held out his right paw.

"Oh...uh sure. Nice to meet ya," offered Sarge, his eyes still focused on the poodle.

"Should we go ahead and start?" asked Jasmine.

"Let's give those two just a little more time," grunted Sarge.

"You mean one!" griped old Max as he trudged into the garage. "You don't even want to know what I had to do to get here."

Every pooch and cat quickly glanced at each other in silence. "All righty then," declared Sarge. "Let's get down to the order of business. Well, uh, what was the business again?"

Bernadette rolled her eyes. "We're here to welcome Trixie and Seymour to the neighborhood." Oleo just stared at everyone and kept quiet.

"Oh yeah, that's right," said Sarge. "Once the young humans start leaving for the daytimes, we usually meet once a full moon, but during the day, when the light is way up high in the sky."

"And what do you talk about in these meetings?" wondered Trixie, gazing at Max.

"Well, we discuss neighborhood matters." Max cleared his throat.

"Like what?" Trixie batted her eyelashes.

"Welcoming new dogs and cats, I guess." The sheepdog coughed.

"And, you know, if any of us dogs or cats care to warn each other about possible dangers," added Bernadette.

"Dangers?" inquired Seymour.

"Yeah, like the time we captured those bad humans," exclaimed a jubilant Juan.

Everyone fell silent. Bernadette and Jasmine stared at each other. The new Elt watched everyone as well, although he had no idea what Juan was talking about. "Well, we kind of stopped a really bad thing from happening, and saved Elt and Bernadette from dog-nappers," boasted Sarge.

"Dog-nappers? Oooh! How exciting!" gushed Trixie. "This is an eventful place to reside in."

"Si. You should see Elt perform his really cool tricks," bragged Juan. "He can run faster than human transport machines."

"Really?" breathed Trixie. "I didn't know that."

"Yeah, Elt. Show these kids some of your really special talents," insisted Sarge.

Oleo didn't know how to react. He opened his mouth slowly, trying to think of an excuse when Bernadette interrupted sharply. "Uh, we don't have time for that. We need to focus on welcoming our new neighbors."

"And of course on meeting the most talented Doberman this side of the Mississippi." Every head turned toward the voice as Prince strutted into the room.

"Now he shows up," grumbled Sarge.

"Better late than never," pronounced Prince, eyes on Trixie, and moving majestically towards her. "Now this meeting is official. My name is Prince, at your service my dear." He nearly bowed before her.

"I do declare," Trixie lauded. She seemed to be out of breath. "But how very handsome you are!"

"I've been trained, groomed, and raised by the finest humans possible," boasted Prince, his eyes raised to the ceiling.

"Oh brother!" cried Bernadette.

"Will there be tea and crumpets served tonight?" inquired Seymour.

"Tea and. . . what?" stuttered Sarge.

"No tea, Seymour, just some tasty biscuits Juan sets out for Chin and Sarge," replied Max.

"I'll bring something for us next time," offered Jasmine. "Unless you'd like to bring those, those crumbles."

"It's crumpets," Seymour clarified. "And yes, I would be honored to bring them."

"Well, before we close the meeting, does anyone have anything to say?" inquired Sarge.

Trixie paused for a few seconds. "Well, our humans are about to travel somewhere, on some type of a trip, but I don't know where, and it seems like they are leaving us behind. We usually travel everywhere with our humans, but something is different this time." What Trixie didn't realize was that her humans were about to embark on a time machine journey into the future.

"I love traveling," Prince cut in. "I can take you to some of the finest establishments in town."

"I think I'm going to throw up," moaned Bernadette.

"Elt, we haven't heard much from you," commented Max.

"Uh, I'm..." started the new Elt.

"He's not feeling like himself," interrupted Bernadette.

"No, I'm definitely not myself," quipped the new Elt. Bernadette pinched her mouth shut to keep from laughing.

"Hmm. Okay then," said Sarge. "Shall we?"

The old timers all turned their attention to the Chow Chow. Then the new neighbors followed suit. Chin opened his eyes. "To travel afar means to travel nowhere," intoned Chin, gravely. The pets all listened to the mysterious words, wondering if there were more. Chin smiled and proceeded to leave the garage.

"I get it," exclaimed the new Elt. "We may think we're going somewhere when we travel, but we really didn't travel that far. To go far would mean to like, travel out of this world." Oleo's explanation was met with silence. It was just a little too advanced for the minds that were gathered in that room.

"I think Chin's back to not making sense again," remarked Jasmine.

"Here, Here," announced Sarge. "Meeting adjourned." Seymour and Trixie watched as the group quietly filed toward the garage door.

"Muchas gracias for coming to mi casa" said Juan.

"Much obliged," twittered Trixie. Then she noticed the new Elt heading out the door. "Yoo hoo, Elt, would you mind walking me home?"

Oleo stopped, glanced at Bernadette, and then turned around to face Trixie. "Uh, walk you?" he questioned.

Trixie now realized there was something strange about Elt. For one, he wasn't continuously staring at her like he had done in their previous encounters. No, something was not the same.

"It would be my highest honor to walk you home Miss Trixie," interjected Prince. "If it's okay with my buddy Elt..."

"Quite alright," Bernadette dismissed him. "Let's go Elt." The new Elt, Bernadette, and Jasmine all exited the garage while Prince prattled on.

"First, let me tell you about the grandest of all my accomplishments," swaggered Prince as he, Trixie, and Seymour followed the rest of the pets. "Wait a second, they're ALL grand. I, I don't know where to begin."

When Bernadette reached her house, Jasmine leaped up on her fence. "Okay, what's going on with you two?" asked the tabby. "He's acting weird, and you're speaking for him."

"I'm not feeling like myself today," repeated the new Elt. "Maybe I'll be more like me when I wake up." At that very moment, something quite unexpected, surprising, and downright unbelievable happened, right in front of Bernadette and Jasmine. As Oleo uttered his last statement, his figure began to disintegrate; he just faded in pieces and vanished. Within seconds, another figure appeared in his place! At first, the new figure appeared snowy, like an old black and white TV, but then a very recognizable figure began to take shape. It was Elt! The real Elt!

"Whoa, what just happened?" Jasmine was stunned.

Bernadette was speechless for a few seconds, but then it dawned on her. She sniffed Elt and then wagged her tail furiously. "You're back!" she exclaimed. "It is you!"

Jasmine didn't know what to do or say. Elt, elated to be home, paced back and forth in front of Bernadette's house a few times. Then he leaped over her fence and back again with ease.

"What was it like?" begged Bernadette. "Where did you go?"

"Now I'm even more confused," moaned Jasmine.

"I'll tell you all about it when we go on our walk," promised Elt. "I really need to get home and make sure my humans are okay."

"Yes, okay," agreed Bernadette. With that, Elt dashed off towards his house, disappearing almost instantly. Bernadette pushed her gate open and entered her yard.

"Wait a minute, can you at least acknowledge what we just witnessed here?" implored Jasmine.

"Yep," called Bernadette over her shoulder. "Elt's back from a mission in outer space, and his replicate, Oleo, is back on board the alien transporter." Bernadette ran away towards her backyard.

Jasmine shook her head. "I must really need some sleep. I'm having some crazy dreams even while I'm still awake." She jumped off her fence and ran through Bernadette's yard, heading for the comfort of Mrs. Reed's back porch.

CHAPTER 10

"COMMENCE TRANSFORMATIONS," DIRECTED MATHEUN AS he pushed a series of buttons on the console. Widenmauer, Myotaur, and Klecktonis faded and disappeared before everyone's eyes. Elt and Sparky waited while Coladeus approached the modules. Matheun monitored their travel on the console screen. "Transformation successful," he announced. "Targets have landed at the proper coordinates."

"Excellent," replied Coladeus. "Now it's time for us to go." Coladeus stepped into one of the modules. He directed Elt to the small module while Sparky climbed into one of the large ones. All three adjusted their masks and tanks. Coladeus glanced over at the two canines. Sparky had been on a mission in outer space before, so he seemed fine. Elt, however, looked a little nervous. Although it couldn't be seen, Elt felt his heart pounding like a bass drum. He nodded to Matheun.

"Commence transformation," directed Matheun once again to his fellow Trianthian, who was manning the transformation device. Each of the three slowly disappeared. Elt experienced and remembered nothing. Before he knew it, he was standing on Titan's surface in fierce wind and driving rain. The three other team members were there waiting uncomfortably in the unstable atmosphere.

Through the rain, the crew could barely see the damaged pipe, protruding from the ground and attached to the water facility. It was hard to detect the crack, for the light on Titan was faint, like a cloudy dusk evening on Earth. The rain made it even harder to view.

Coladeus motioned for Sparky to come his way. The Trianthian hopped on the Golden Retriever's back, and in a flash, Sparky flew the Trianthian to the top of the structure. The glow from Coladeus' body emitted enough light for the crew to see where the repair was needed.

It was time for Widenmauer to initiate things. Fighting the nasty weather, the creature crawled up the pipe, like a six-legged spider, all the way to the affected area. Widenmauer began to spin a web-like substance into the crack of the pipe. The substance acted like an adhesive, much like glue on a school project. By the time Widenmauer was finished, the polluted water that was seeping from the crack had just about ceased.

Sparky left Coladeus at the top of the structure, surrounded the pipeline with the rope that he brought, and then flew down to assist Elt and Myotaur. The retriever noticed Elt couldn't let go of the pipe, so he tugged on the rope while Elt and Myotaur pushed with all their might. The rain caused the ground to be muddy, so it was difficult for them to keep their footing, but finally the pipe that had been leaning, causing the breakage, slowly straightened into place.

The big blue giant nodded at the dogs before letting go. He retrieved a heavy boulder that was nearby. Without Myotaur, Elt strained to use all of his super strength to keep the pipe straight. In a moment, Myotaur had placed the rock up against the pipe to brace it and prevent it from ever leaning again. "Whew," panted Elt, shaking the rain out of his eyes.

Meanwhile, Widenmauer, who had crept back down from the crack to the surface, carried Klecktonis back up to the repair site. Klecktonis focused on the partly mended crack. In mere seconds, her scorching eyes melted the web-like substance deep into the crack, much like a hot glue gun on a broken toy. The leaking stopped altogether.

With the crack mended and the pipe straightened, the mission was a success. Coladeus motioned for Sparky, but Widenmauer climbed to the top of the pipe. Coladeus shared a ride down the structure with Klecktonis.

Myotaur and the two canines met the others at the base of the pipe. They trekked over to the entrance of the Tsarian living quarters, which was situated about five-hundred feet from the water plant. Before they walked inside, they noticed something strange. Through the haze of the rain and wind, two small mini jet-like vehicles emerged from behind the river. Elt squinted to see who the travelers were. Were they Tsarian police forces just on patrol? Were they making sure that the strangers were there on a peaceful mission?

As they approached, the group could see through the jet windows that the pilots' skin-tone was more of a yellowish hue, unlike the greenish glow of the Trianthians. Their heads were shaped like diamonds, and they possessed large, white eyes. Elt and Sparky didn't know what to expect, but Coladeus did.

The jets flew suddenly away from the Tsarian camp just as the doors to the Tsarian living quarters opened. The aliens welcomed Coladeus and his crew. The Tsarian group leader gave the team a quick tour of their quarters, which provided Elt and the rest of the team a chance to dry off and remove their masks.

Although Coladeus was humbled by the Tsarian gratitude, it was evident that the Trianthian leader was concerned. Just before it was time to transport back to Trianthius I, Widenmauer communicated to Coladeus in private. Coladeus nodded in agreement.

Elt was still overwhelmed with the incredible events of the day. He had become a member of a galactic team of superheroes confronted with a challenge: to repair a weakened water pipe that threatened the survival of a civilization attempting to colonize one of Saturn's moons.

Coladeus checked a small instrument that he pulled out of his pouch. He pushed a tiny, red button and placed the device back in his pouch. "It is time," he announced. The crew slipped their masks back on and left the building. The rain had ceased, but the wind still swirled.

Sparky, Elt, and Coladeus were the first ones to be transported back to Trianthius I. Minutes later, Elt and Sparky watched from the transport area as their teammates' bodies materialized. Matheun greeted the group and adjusted his distransulator. He spoke first to Coladeus, who quickly left the room. Matheun shared the message with all the members separately, finishing with Elt and Sparky. "We will now meet in the briefing room while we're en route to Earth," stated Matheun. "Please leave your equipment in this room."

Everyone dropped their masks, placed their tanks on the floor, and followed the first officer. In the briefing room, everyone found a place to rest. Two Trianthians served refreshments to the famished crew. Then the door hummed and Coladeus stepped into the room. He moved to the podium and adjusted his distransulator.

"I want to thank you all for your diligent work and commitment to complete the mission," announced Coladeus with pride. "The Tsarian people are very grateful, knowing their water supply is safe and that they won't have to construct a new pipeline. They have you to thank for that." Coladeus paused a moment before continuing. "Trianthius I is traveling at a very fast pace and should arrive at Earth in about four Earth hours. We will then proceed to Venus to drop off our next crew member." Coladeus stepped away from the podium. Sparky raised his right paw.

"What is your question, Sparky?" asked Coladeus.

"Who were those dudes in those flying machines?" asked the Golden Retriever. "Were those Tsarians too?"

Coladeus considered his answer for a few seconds before answering simply, "I'm afraid not." Klecktonis and Myotaur watched the canines. They didn't understand what Sparky was saying, but they could sense what he was talking about. They knew who those aliens were.

"They are a species of unfriendly foes that have threatened many civilizations for thousands of duraceps," continued Coladeus. "They are the Quadrasones, the one true enemy of the Trianthians."

"So, what were they doing on Titan?" inquired Elt.

"I'm not quite sure," replied Coladeus, honestly. "The Quadrasones are a very aggressive species. They would rather destroy than build."

Widenmauer spoke to Coladeus in his native speech. Coladeus once again nodded in approval. "Widenmauer just reminded me," he added, "Based upon his inspection of that crack in the pipeline, he believes that it was deliberate, not natural. So the Quadrasones could be responsible for that damaged pipe."

"Do they take over what they destroy?" wondered Sparky.

Coladeus paused. "No, they destroy, take what they think is useful to them, and then move on. They do have a keen interest in ruining civilizations that Trianthians support. Once again, they are our only true enemy."

As Trianthius I soared towards Earth, Elt had a short time to reflect on the mission. For one, he was able to travel through space, something that no ordinary canine would ever do. Second, he worked with some incredible individuals from other worlds. And last, he had met a new friend, Sparky. Would this be the first and last time he worked with Sparky and the others? It would be very difficult to visit the Golden Retriever, for he didn't live near San Francisco.

Just about the time Elt was closing his eyes, a Trianthian crew member entered and pointed toward the door. Elt guessed it was time to leave. The pooch scanned the room one last time. Myotaur and Widenmauer were resting, so he didn't want to disturb them. Klecktonis acknowledged Elt with a nod of her head. Sparky walked over to Elt. He held up his right paw for one final paw bump. "It was awesome working with you, dude."

Elt paw bumped his new friend. "Do you think we'll ever work together again?"

"Sooner than you think." Sparky's eyes twinkled.

Elt followed the Trianthian back into the elevator. He was once again escorted to the transport modules where Matheun stood at the console. Matheun looked up, adjusted his language device and approached Elt.

"Elt, we are going to transport you via the modules, like we did on Titan," said the first officer. "We will first transfer Oleo here, to Trianthius I; then we will send you to wherever Oleo's coordinates were. At the moment, it appears that Oleo is with one member of your species and one other, not a human."

Elt thought for a few seconds. What would Oleo be doing with another canine and no humans? He then remembered. "Is it light or dark on that part of Earth right now?" asked Elt.

Matheun checked his computer. "It is dark, in the middle of one of your Earth nights."

"The neighborhood meeting," nodded Elt to himself. "That's where he is. OK." Elt took a deep breath and walked toward the modules. Before he stepped up to the platform, Matheun approached Elt. He bent down, twisted Elt's collar, and removed the stone. He produced a heftier stone from his pouch and showed it to Elt. This stone contained a slight, yellow button which protruded from the stone. Matheun then affixed the stone to Elt's collar.

"The Captain feels that this stone may assist you in your quest to fly in the future," explained Matheun. "And if your human needs to contact us, he can push the button on the stone." Matheun straightened up. "Isn't technology wonderful?" he grinned.

Just then a Trianthian crew member alerted Matheun. The first officer nodded toward Elt. "It is time. Please step into the module." Elt stepped inside and waited. "We have Oleo's coordinates," related Matheun. Then he paused and locked eyes with the super dog. "We shall see you again, Elt from Earth. Commence transmission."

Elt watched Matheun. He heard a noise that came from the module next to him. All of a sudden, Oleo appeared in his true form. The next few seconds were a blur. When Elt opened his eyes, he stood in front of Bernadette and Jasmine, right in front of the Cocker Spaniel's front yard.

CHAPTER 11

IT TOOK A FEW MINUTES for Ralph to realize what was happening. It had happened so many mornings before this, that the boy thought it was a dream. First, there was one lick. Then there was a second, third, and multitudes of doggie kisses on Ralph's face. When his eyes finally opened, he couldn't believe what he saw.

But was he sure? In about a day and a half, Oleo had performed some really incredible feats. Although they noticed indifferences in Elt, Jenny and Mr. Eltison didn't detect Oleo as an Elt replacement. In fact, Oleo had made Ralph's day without Elt more pleasant than the boy could have ever imagined. "Is it you, Elt?" hoped Ralph.

Elt was wriggling with excitement. He had enjoyed the mission. He had loved the adventure of saving a civilization and meeting strange new beings from other worlds, but his number one job was Ralph.

Ralph twisted Elt's collar. There was still a stone attached to the collar's underside, but it looked different. It seemed larger, and there was some kind of a button on it. Ralph was afraid to touch the button.

He didn't want Elt to disappear, or to cause any alarm. "How did you get here?" wondered Ralph. "And where's Oleo?"

Ralph wasn't sure if Elt understood what he was asking him. At that moment, it really didn't matter. Elt had returned! But had Coladeus brought him and had Ralph missed it? Ralph knew nothing about the new transporting method.

Ralph hopped out of bed and hurried into the kitchen. Mr. Eltison was drinking a cup of coffee while reading the Herald newspaper. He gazed up and spotted Ralph at the kitchen doorway. "Hey, whatever you said to Elt yesterday worked," said Ralph's dad as he showed Ralph the newspaper. "Right here on my chair."

Elt padded up to Ralph's side. The boy smiled at his dog and patted his head. "He wasn't feeling well yesterday. He's much more himself today."

Ralph's dad smiled. "That's good." He motioned toward the stove. "I cooked some eggs. You want some?"

"Sure," Ralph replied. The boy reached into the pantry and scooped up a helping of Elt's dry dog food, but stopped while the scoop was still in the bag. Dropping it, he reached for a can of moist canned food and then went for the can opener.

"This is a special day," announced Ralph to Elt. Elt wagged his tail. "Brace your noses," announced Ralph. He opened the can and dumped the moist food into his dog's bowl. Mr. Eltison laughed as he watched his son hold his nose and dump the food at the same time.

Elt, nothing like Oleo when it came to liking dog food, devoured the moist food in less than a minute. The smell disappeared with the food. "Is it okay if I go swimming with Jenny today?" asked Ralph as he washed his hands.

"I don't see why not," answered Ralph's dad. "Do you have any chores to finish?"

"Just a little mess in my room," said Ralph. "I think she'll call me soon."

Ralph knew that Elt and Bernadette weren't allowed at the pool, but he had spoken with Jenny the day before. He didn't realize that Elt would return this soon. He wanted to spend some time with his dog. "Maybe we can still walk later," thought Ralph. "I'll talk to Jenny while we're swimming."

When Ralph arrived at Jenny's house, he noticed Caroline playing in her yard. He valued his time with Jenny, but he wasn't sure if the kids next door were able to go swimming at the neighborhood pool. Jenny opened the door. "Come on in," she said.

Ralph followed Jenny inside. "Hey, do you think we should invite Bryan and Caroline today?"

"Sure, it will be fun," answered Jenny.

The two kids walked over to the fence that divided the Rodgers's and the Greenlee's yards. Caroline was playing with a large moving box in the side yard. Bryan was handing her a big roll of tape. He noticed the two kids at the fence. "Hey, do you want to go swimming with us?" inquired Jenny.

Bryan dropped the roll of tape, smiled at Caroline, and dashed over to the back door. "Hey Mum," yelled Bryan. Caroline dropped the one end of the box and followed her brother. A few minutes later, both Caroline and Bryan ran out of the back door with their bathing suits on. With towels draped over their necks, the kids scaled the fence and jumped down into Jenny's yard. "We can go for two hours," puffed Bryan.

"That's about how long we'll stay," smiled Jenny. "Let's go." The four kids started down Valleydale Drive.

"Hey, what were you working on in your yard?" asked Ralph.

"We were constructing a time machine, just like me dad," laughed Caroline.

"Cool," admired Jenny. "I read about the time machine. That's so exciting."

"Want to know a secret?" Bryan was bursting with eagerness.

"No!" exclaimed Caroline. "We're not supposed to tell."

"The whole world is going to know by tomorrow," said Bryan.

Caroline rolled her eyes and shook her head in disbelief.

"Next week, when the time machine travels into the future," Bryan half-whispered, "me and me sister will be on it with our dad."

Jenny and Ralph stopped walking.

"You mean *you're* gonna travel in time? Just like in all those books and movies?" Ralph was dumbfounded.

"Yeah," answered Bryan, whose grin couldn't have been bigger. "I believe twenty-five years into the future, here in Spring Valley."

"Our mum doesn't want to go," added Caroline, deciding to join all the excitement. "She didn't want to travel unless it's on a real holiday. So guess who's going with us?"

Ralph, being the adventure-loving boy that he was, hoped that the kids would ask him right there on the spot. But it wasn't to be. "You remember Mr. Buttersample, the candy man?" asked Bryan. Jenny and Ralph stared at each other, then back at the British kids.

"We love that place," chattered Jenny. "But I haven't been back since he gave us that tour on opening day."

"Well," said Caroline, "We did go back, and Dad asked him to travel with us."

"And he's going to bring all kinds of candy with him," interjected Bryan. "We're going to see what his candy shop looks like in the future."

What the kids told Ralph and Jenny was true. On the night of Professor Van Hausen's offer to Greenlee, Stanley had returned home with the exciting news. Mrs. Greenlee knew that her husband wanted to travel in the time machine, but she was worried about the kids. Was there any danger? Could they get hurt? Were the kids experienced enough to handle emergency situations?

Greenlee had assured his wife that although there were some dangers associated with the actual process of time travel, there had been three successful trial runs on the time machine already. The trip with the kids was going to be simple; travel twenty-five years into the future and be back home in one hour. What could go wrong?

Mrs. Greenlee had finally agreed, but on one condition; she wanted to be right beside Professor Van Hausen, to make sure that Stanley and the kids made it back safely. That meant she wanted to stay and not travel. "I want to know where you are and how you will get back safely," said Mrs. Greenlee firmly.

Stanley had been a little disappointed, but understood her concerns. Although she supported him whole-heartedly, time travel was not on her "to do" list, and she wanted Stanley, Bryan, and Caroline back in one piece, one hour after the launch.

So, then had come the decision of who to invite in Mrs. Greenlee's place. The professors Van Hausen and Greenlee thought about holding a sweepstakes drawing for the final ticket, but then reconsidered, for there was plenty of time for that after the first successful run into the future.

The next morning, before he started work, Greenlee had promised his kids a trip to Buttersample's. He had been working very long hours and wanted to spend some quality time with the children.

The Greenlees were welcomed by Henry Buttersample, who customarily greeted his guests in the front lobby of his candy shop and factory. Business had still been booming since opening day. Folks from Spring Valley and beyond filled their carts with abundant heaps of sweet, delicious treats. The Greenlees' interaction with Henry was brief, but to the point. The conversation had barely started when Bryan "spilled the beans" about traveling on the time machine.

"That's wonderful news!" Henry Buttersample had exclaimed. "What a treat to visit the future! If it were me, I'd go and see how exciting our candy emporium will become."

"Dad!" Caroline had a great idea. "Can Mr. Buttersample travel with us so he can see his candy shop in the future?"

Professor Greenlee smiled. "I'm not sure if Mr. Buttersample would really want to venture out into the future. He's such a busy man running this delectable establishment."

Henry looked interested. "Actually, the idea sounds fascinating. In fact, our family has discussed the possibility of one day traveling on your time machine."

"Very well then, Mr. Buttersample, it looks like you're coming with us," a grinning Professor Greenlee remarked. The kids were elated.

As the Greenlee children told their story to Ralph and Jenny, they entered the gates of the swimming pool. Jenny and Ralph couldn't believe it! The time machine news was all abuzz! But as soon as they saw the slide and diving board, their attention was diverted. Within seconds, their towels dropped and they all either jumped or slid into the pool. They played and swam for their full two hours.

On the way home from the pool, just before they parted ways, the kids stopped in front of the Greenlee's house. "Will you be there at the launching?" asked Bryan.

"We wouldn't miss it for the world," answered Jenny. Ralph nodded his head in agreement.

Later that evening, Ralph and Jenny walked their dogs. They didn't invite the Greenlee children, for they wanted a little alone time with their dogs. Besides, the Greenlee kids ate dinner out with their parents that evening.

Bernadette was relieved to see Elt again. The night before had been a "shock and leave" moment, when Oleo and Elt suddenly switched places, and then Elt took off for his human's house.

There was no lemonade break, for it was getting late in the day. Ralph and Elt needed to head home and help Mr. Eltison prepare dinner. Bernadette was disappointed that she never had the chance to ask Elt about his mission. She had so many questions for him, like where did you go? What did you do? And who did you travel with? Those questions would have to wait.

Ralph's dad decided to eat at Brown's for dinner. It had been a couple of weeks since they had frequented their favorite Friday night stop, so Mr. Eltison and Ralph jumped into the truck and ventured downtown.

When Ralph returned, he quickly showered and spent some quality play time with Elt. He had missed Elt, even though his dog was only gone one and a half days. Ralph was exhausted from both the swim and the walk. Elt was still a little fatigued from his voyage to Titan. Both of them were soon ready to pass into a deep slumber. Before Ralph fell asleep, however, he once again checked Elt's collar. He felt the small button that protruded from the stone, and then released the collar. Ralph fell asleep within minutes.

In order to treat his family to dinner that evening, Professor Greenlee had returned home from the lab early, leaving Van Hausen, busy with event preparation and Edward, preparing the end of day readings and completing some technical prep work for the upcoming trip. Their family dinner was relaxing and refreshing and they returned home happy.

"Kids," admonished Mr. Greenlee shortly after arriving home, "you need to get plenty of rest." He kissed both of them on the forehead. "It's time to head to bed." Bryan and Caroline hugged him, then hurried to their rooms. It was difficult for the Greenlee children to fall asleep that night, even though they too, were exhausted from the swimming.

In just three days, they were going to travel where no child had ever ventured before.

Meanwhile that evening, Professor Van Hausen was very busy preparing for the launch day celebrations. A humongous stage had been erected in an open area on campus, just outside the laboratory. A monstrous screen, almost sixty feet in height, was built so folks outside could witness the launch. Every folding chair on campus was re-located to the site in front of the stage.

There were stations from which members of the newspaper, television, and radio stations could broadcast live. Mr. and Mrs. Brown, along with other restaurant owners in Spring Valley, would set up booths, much like a carnival, to serve those who got hungry waiting for the launch. Refreshments of all varieties had to be present, for there would be folks from all around the world who would attend.

Van Hausen still confirmed the final adjustments with Stanley and Edward each day, but he relied on the two of them for all of the technical data. He was too busy making sure the publicity and promotions for the launch were complete. By the end of the day, Van Hausen was exhausted. He retired about nine o'clock in the evening, long after Professor Greenlee had already headed home. "Please lock up when you leave, Edward," he said, closing the door behind him.

"I will Professor." Edward checked the console's final readings for the day. When he looked up, he made doubly sure the professor had left for good, and then placed the clipboard down and licked his lips. He reached out and began to input new numbers into the computer.

The time machine's engines rumbled to life. Edward set the date and time for departure. He also instructed the time machine to automatically return in one half hour. He then pushed the last set of buttons. He opened the door to the time machine, sat down, and closed the door. The platform began to spin.

Luckily, no one was in the building. Edward knew that security wouldn't arrive until around eleven, so no one was there to hear the noisy take-off. Within seconds, the time machine disappeared; all that remained was the steam from the launching.

CHAPTER 12

"Is it time to go yet?" asked Ralph impatiently. Ralph's dad checked his watch.

"The launch is at two," answered Mr. Eltison. "We still have some time." Ralph was beyond excited. The boy wished he was the one traveling in the time machine that day, but he was elated that his new friends would have the chance. Maybe it would be him some day.

"When can we leave?" he asked.

"I talked to Jenny's mom. She's getting off work early today, around eleven-thirty, so she'll pick up Jenny and head home. She said to come over around twelve-fifteen, and then we can leave together."

"Can I bring Elt?" asked the boy.

"We will be outdoors, and Elt usually demonstrates excellent behavior when he's at public events," answered Ralph's dad. "I don't see why not, but he's your responsibility."

"Excellent!" Ralph hugged Elt. "We're going to see history, boy!"

The whole town of Spring Valley was abuzz, for in just a few short hours, history was about to be made. The little town was being overrun with thousands of visitors. Spring Valley, being dubbed by news reporters local and far as "Time Town" and "Spring Time Valley," didn't hold many motels or hotels, so Professor Van Hausen used a few of his buildings on campus as make-shift residences for out-of-towners. Still, some folks had to find lodging in neighboring towns, including Bordertown.

Earlier that morning, Professor Greenlee ate a hearty breakfast with his family. A pre-launch feast of his kids' favorite pancakes and sausage was on the menu, courtesy of Mrs. Greenlee. Then the family left together early, for not only did they want to beat the traffic, Professor Greenlee had to assist Edward and Professor Van Hausen with last minute details concerning the launch.

At both Bryan's and Caroline's requests, Trixie and Seymour accompanied the family to the laboratory. They would remain inside, in an office just outside the lab, but close enough to give a lick or nudge of encouragement to their young human travelers. Mrs. Greenlee would watch over them while the kids and Stanley were gone.

Professor Van Hausen, although quite exhausted from all of the ceremonial details, was as excited and vibrant as ever on the morning of the launch. He was quite confident, having traveled three times before on his time machine, and he was sure the trip would fare his travelers well. In just a few hours, his name would be as famous as Einstein's.

Van Hausen hadn't slept a wink the night before; his mind was full of excitement. When he arrived, the laboratory showed signs of someone having been there earlier, but no one was there now. The door was locked, and the security guard was at his post. "Surely Edward must be here somewhere," thought Van Hausen to himself. But he still saw no one.

About an hour later, the Greenlees arrived. Van Hausen was relieved to see a majority of his travel team there at the lab. "Have you seen Edward this morning?" he asked.

"No sir, we just arrived," answered Greenlee. The kids, Mrs. Greenlee, Trixie, and Seymour were ushered into the next room by an associate from the campus. "The kids are very excited."

"And so am I." Van Hausen appeared triumphant. "This day is going to be a glorious day, a day your kids will remember for the rest of their lives."

The final time traveler, Henry Buttersample, arrived on campus with his family. His wife and kids were nervous, but excited. Along with his family, Henry brought goodies from his candy emporium. Some of the treats would be given away free, others were to be set up for sale when the crowds arrived. Professor Greenlee had instructed Henry to meet him in the laboratory. Once Henry dropped his family off and said his good-byes, he reported to the lab.

The crowds had begun to form early. Some folks spent the night and waited in line, for they wanted to sit in the front row. Mayor Helms, named the Master of Ceremonies for the launch, assisted with the crowd control.

Ralph, his dad, and Elt drove away from the house ten minutes after twelve. As they drove up to Jenny's house, Jenny, her mom, and Bernadette exited their home. "Follow me," instructed Mr. Eltison. Ms. Rodgers gave Mr. Eltison the "thumbs up" sign as she and her family found their seats. They drove down Valleydale Drive and Schoolhouse Road, en route to the campus on Observatory Road.

When they arrived at the campus, Mr. Eltison and Ms. Rodgers parked their vehicles. Their cars were just two of thousands stretched in every empty parking area and field on campus. "Wow, it's totally crowded," commented Ralph as they exited their vehicles. Throngs of people were walking toward the seating area. When the Eltisons and the Rodgers' reached the stage, they were seated about fifty rows back, but in the center aisle. The parents, kids, and pets sat down. Elt and Bernadette found spaces near their humans' feet.

Bernadette still hadn't had the chance to ask Elt about the mission, and although she only sat inches from him, she didn't utter a sound, for she didn't want to startle the audience around her.

Meanwhile, inside the lab, Professor Van Hausen asked once again, "Has anyone seen Edward? It's not like him to be late or not show up, especially on this day." Edward's disappearance was strange indeed, but with so much happening, trying to locate him in such a short period of time was out of the question. He was supposed to be preparing the time machine for the launch, and he was to take charge of the console when the trip commenced. Edward's disappearance now meant that Van Hausen would definitely have to monitor the controls, something he hadn't performed before. He had been the passenger in the earlier trials.

Van Hausen was both worried about his co-worker and disappointed in him. They had shared the whole time machine process together, from invention to launch. Now the big day had arrived without Edward. But Van Hausen didn't know how Edward really felt; shoved out of the way and replaced by Professor Greenlee.

"I'll ask one of my graduate students to assist me," announced Van Hausen. "She can watch things when I have to step out, but I'll be here for the time machine's departure and arrival."

"I can work on all the preliminaries," offered Professor Greenlee. "Go ahead, we're fine here. Just be back to launch us."

"Thank you, Stanley."

Bryan and Caroline kept busy by reading and playing with their pets in the side office. They knew it would be time to go when their dad appeared. "What time is it Mum?" asked Caroline.

"It's close to one," answered Mrs. Greenlee.

Professor Greenlee began the pre-launch inspection of the time machine. He first checked the physical structure of the machine. Everything checked okay, not even a scratch. The professor read the time meter on the time machine's computer.

"Something's not right here," frowned Greenlee to himself as he examined Edward's reports. "The hour and minute readings don't exactly match what's written on his report." Greenlee called Van Hausen, but the professor didn't answer. Stanley didn't know what to think. Was there a problem with the time meter? "This is kind of strange. The device is here, in excellent shape," thought Greenlee. "I can't imagine this small error to affect our trip at all, but I'll keep an eye on it." Professor Greenlee put the error out of his mind and never thought to inform Van Hausen.

Once the grad student arrived, Greenlee knew it was time to report to the stage for the pre-launch ceremony. Henry Buttersample called his wife, made sure everything was running smoothly at their candy booth, and then headed to the office in order to accompany the professor and his family to the stage.

Caroline and Bryan hugged their mom, and then their pets. "Let me know what the future is like, kids," said a weeping Mrs. Greenlee. She wiped a few tears from her eyes, but urged her kids to move on.

Just then, Henry Buttersample strode into the office. "It's the candy man!" declared Bryan. Both kids ran to greet him.

"Hey kids, are you ready to see Spring Valley twenty-five years into the future?" asked Henry. Both kids grinned and nodded yes.

"Let's go kids," directed Professor Greenlee as he stuck his head inside the office window. He hugged and kissed Mrs. Greenlee before they exited.

The professor, the kids, and Henry headed outside towards the stage to meet the crowds that were applauding their trip into the future. They would be introduced publicly to the fans, just like astronauts before the launching of a rocket or space shuttle. Elt wasn't quite sure what was happening, but he knew that it was something enormous that brought all of the humans to that one place in Spring Valley.

Mayor Helms stepped up to the podium. This event was by far the most important function ever held in Spring Valley. "Welcome citizens of Spring Valley. Today history will be made in our great little town." The crowd cheered and waved. Television, radio, and internet stations broadcasted the event live.

After the mayor's speech, Mayor Helms introduced Professor Van Hausen. The professor received rousing applause that brought tears to his eyes. "Many years ago, I dreamed of a day like today," he reminisced. "I hoped one day it would come true, and now here we are."

Van Hausen spoke for a few moments more before the time travelers arrived on stage. Once Professor Greenlee, Bryan, Caroline, and Henry Buttersample walked onto the stage, there was an unyielding frenzy of clapping, cheers, and photographer's flashbulbs. Ralph and Jenny clapped and cheered when their friends were announced. Everyone in front of them was standing, so it was easier for the kids to watch the big screen instead of the actual stage.

"So what's the first thing you kids are going to do when you land twenty-five years into the future?" asked Mayor Helms.

"See what kind of candy is at Buttersample's," cried Bryan. Caroline nodded her head in agreement. Henry laughed and clapped his hands in response to their answer.

"Professor Greenlee, do you have any final words before the launch," asked the mayor.

"To my wife, I love her," replied Greenlee. "And I'll return home in time to cut the grass tonight." The crowd laughed and clapped at his answer.

"And now it's time for our time travelers to make their way back to the time machine," announced Mayor Helms.

"And I will be leaving for the laboratory as well, to make sure we have a successful launch," interjected Van Hausen.

As the now famous group left the stage, the Spring Valley High School Band performed some patriotic tunes for the audience. There were even a few local speakers and a rock band ready to perform on stage before the launch.

As the time travelers re-entered the laboratory, Henry Buttersample stopped, for there was something he wanted to say. "Professor, May I address our group?"

"What is it, chap?" asked Greenlee.

"We're about to embark on something spectacular. And so, I'd like to show you something I've been working on for a very long time, even before I opened the candy emporium." The kids' eyes grew almost two times their size. They knew it must have something to do with candy. Stanley watched the excitement on his children's faces.

Henry reached into his pocket and pulled out two pieces of candy wrapped in silver paper, lined with red stripes and yellow stars. "I was going to wait until after we returned," said Henry. "But what the heck, I figure now's as good a time as ever."

Caroline jumped for joy, while Bryan placed his hands on his cheeks. Henry handed them each a piece of the candy. "It's my new invention," claimed Henry. "I call it the Wonder Candy, but I'm not sure if that's what I really want to name it."

The kids didn't know how to react. "What flavor is it?" asked Bryan.

"Is it chewy or crunchy?" wondered Caroline. "Is it gum or chocolate?"

"Yes," answered Henry. "Wonder Candy has an assortment of flavors, and it's both chewy and crunchy. It ends up as bubble gum."

"Can we open it?" insisted Bryan.

"I was hoping to open them when we return home," replied Henry. "You know, kind of like a celebration."

"That makes perfect sense, Mr. Buttersample," agreed Professor Greenlee. "Kids, put them in your pockets and eat them later." The kids obediently stuffed the candy into their pockets.

"It's time," announced Professor Greenlee.

"Did you hear that?" teased a smiling Henry. "He said TIME." The group walked into the laboratory, the kids following their dad. The kids marveled at the time machine's size and shape. Professor Van Hausen walked straight towards the console and scanned some numbers on the screen. Then he gazed up at the four travelers in front of him.

"Professor Van Hausen, we are ready to travel," declared Professor Greenlee.

"Edward doesn't know what he's missing," Van Hausen said resolutely. A campus staff associate approached Van Hausen and whispered a message into the professor's ear. Van Hausen nodded and the associate moved away.

"I've just been informed that we go live in five minutes," announced Van Hausen. Only one camera technician and one reporter were allowed in the laboratory. Through them, the broadcast would be aired to all of the television and internet networks.

"Let's get ready children," directed Greenlee. He opened the door to the time machine and allowed Caroline to step in first, followed by Bryan. They sat down in the two back seats while the older men sat down in the front. The four travelers buckled up and prepared their oxygen masks. Greenlee checked his children's masks for proper oxygen availability. He then gave Van Hausen the "thumbs up" sign.

"Five...four...three...two...one..." echoed the television producer via a speaker in the lab. The camera technician focused in on the reporter, and then shifted directly to the four travelers inside the time machine. The announcer talked briefly to the children, then Buttersample, and finally Greenlee. Last of all, Van Hausen stepped in and wrapped up the pre-launch interviews.

"I'm afraid at this time, I need to position myself at the control console to prepare for the launch," he concluded.

Now the pre-launch ceremonies were over. Outside, the Eltisons and Rodgers were among the throngs of folks waiting and watching for the time machine to skyrocket into the future.

Inside the lab, Van Hausen continued the preparations. "Now Professor, correct me if I'm wrong, but our coordinates will have you landing at the park, yes?"

"Yes. Hopefully nothing has changed at the park in the next twenty-five years," remarked Greenlee.

"We'll see you in an hour." Van Hausen smiled confidently.

The four voyagers placed their oxygen masks over their mouths. The children positioned goggles over their eyes, just as a precautionary measure. The whole world watched as Professor Van Hausen started the time machine's engines. The platform began to rotate. The machine began to spin, faster and faster. The steam poured into the lab.

The folks outside and around the world watched in awe as the machine's hum transformed into a roar. Through the billowing steam, folks could only now see a blur, for the time machine whirled in an endless flurry.

Searing light suddenly blazed into the room and then BAM! Some startled gasps came from the onlookers, while everyone still strained to see through the steam swirling on the screen. A wondering hush fell over the crowd. When the smoke cleared, a collective murmur rose up into deafening amazement. The time machine and its inhabitants had disappeared! Van Hausen quickly came on screen and reassured the world that the launch had been successful. The crowd outside erupted into a harmonious, earsplitting cheer.

Caroline opened her eyes. During the rapid, bumpy ride, she had kept her eyes closed. Her brother, on the other hand, watched the virtual, countless series of forward rotations around the earth.

Now the trip had ended. The time machine had landed. Caroline glanced over at Bryan. He ripped off his oxygen mask, goggles, and seatbelt. He was ready to jump out of the time machine, but waited for his father's approval.

Henry and Stanley removed their masks. As the dust and debris cleared, the travelers noticed that they had indeed landed somewhere in the park. Their landing area included a small field nestled between two stretches of tall pine trees.

"Our legs might be a little wobbly," announced Greenlee. "Give them time if you need." Henry waited for the professor to make the first move. Once Greenlee stepped out of the time machine, the candy entrepreneur followed. His legs were a bit shaky, but he managed. The kids jumped out of the time machine with no trouble. Maybe it was due to their size, but the trip didn't affect them at all.

Once the group passed the landing area, the woods and fields cleared away much sooner than expected. It was Greenlee's understanding that they would land deep in the park's forest, but something wasn't right. Even though these four travelers were relatively new to Spring Valley, they did know that scores of trees surrounded the park's lake. But what they saw now were rows of houses, condominiums, and townhouses encompassing the body of water. In the distance, they could see skyscrapers that filled the once quaint Main Street. There were giant cranes erecting a new one.

"Is this Spring Valley, Dad?" wondered Bryan.

"I'm not sure, Son" answered Professor Greenlee quietly. Henry stared silently at all of the new construction before them.

"It is Spring Valley," boomed a condescending voice from behind the group. The travelers whirled around to see a welcoming committee of five men sauntering up to the group. Both Professor Greenlee and Henry Buttersample knew the leader's voice, but they couldn't believe it.

"You're just in time," laughed the strange man, "to see MY Spring Valley."

"You!" exclaimed both Henry and Stanley simultaneously.

CHAPTER 13

"WHO'S THAT MAN, DAD?" QUESTIONED Caroline, nervously.

"Why he's my co-worker, Edward...Edward Livingstone," answered Professor Greenlee in disbelief.

"Actually, it's *Professor* Livingstone now." Edward grinned maliciously. "And, oh yes, soon to be *Mayor* Livingstone."

Henry rushed forward and confronted Edward. "You arrived just before I closed my doors on opening day."

"Yes I did," remarked Edward. "Oh, and I forgot one more of my titles...Candy Entrepreneur, Inventor of the Wonder Candy!"

"That's MY candy!" blasted Henry. "*I* invented the Wonder Candy!"

"You did twenty-five years ago," Edward's voice was syrupy sweet. "But I changed all of that." From behind Edward, two of the men approached. Henry had seen these men before, too. In fact, the old Spring Valley dealt with these two foes twenty-five years ago.

"Allow me to introduce two of my newest associates," announced Edward. "My two new business partners, Frake and Jake."

"Those are Walter Crum's men!" Henry was astonished. They just went to jail two months ago."

"Well, no," Edward corrected patiently. "These men served their time in prison. And I was there the day they were released back into society."

"You mean...?" asked Stanley.

"Exactly, Professor," interrupted Edward. "I used the time machine a few times, changed a little future history, and viola! All of this is now called 'Livingstonia.'"

"I knew those readings were off," Stanley gritted his teeth.

"Yes, but you weren't in charge of those readings," gloated Edward. "Only I knew the exact readings. That was my job!"

Two more burly men walked up to Edward. "And here are two of my assistants: Fred and Zeb. Let's take you all on a tour. You do want to know what happened to Spring Valley, am I correct?" Fred and Zeb turned and headed straight for the time machine.

"Where are they going?" demanded Henry.

"Oh, they're going to disengage the time machine," smirked Edward.

"But you can't! We're going back to see Mommy today," wailed Caroline.

Edward walked over to Caroline. He bent down so she could hear him clearly. "I'm sorry my dear, but you guys and gal aren't going anywhere soon."

Edward, Frake, and Jake ushered the four time travelers downtown. They passed by rows of houses and businesses, which used to be part of the park, and then crossed over to Main Street. All of the old-style facades on Main Street were gone, replaced by modern skyscrapers and a monorail system.

As they crossed the street, Henry noticed that his old business was still there, but in a new structure. Its name...Livingstone's Wonder Candy Emporium.

"I bet you want to go inside and see my new candy wonderland," chuckled Edward. He could hardly contain his glee.

"How did you steal my business?" demanded Henry. "And where's Mr. Crum? Surely he's behind all of this madness."

"Actually, when I approached you that evening about your wonder candy," related Edward, "I considered contacting Mr. Crum about the idea. But then I thought; who needs that old, crumbled relic? I have access to the time machine. I can do this myself. Well, with a little help." Edward smiled at Frake and Jake.

"Yes Mr. Livingstone," responded Frake, his grin still as creepy as it was twenty-five years before. By jumping ahead first ten, and then twenty-five years, Edward hadn't aged at all.

"So you jumped in time ten years, picked up these two gents, and then jumped again fifteen more, and all of this changed?" asked Stanley.

"I tweaked some things, yeah, you can say that," replied Edward. "Actually I started things fifteen years ago, left, and returned just this morning. It's as if I never left. It's truly amazing."

"I don't get it, are we really stuck here?" worried Bryan.

"I'm afraid so," answered his dad. "With the time machine being disengaged, we can't travel anywhere."

Edward opened the door to his candy emporium. The whole group entered. The store and factory were even bigger than before. The whole first floor was the store, the second floor the factory. Henry was astounded. "How can this be?" he wondered.

"You did give it its start," replied Edward. "But when I marketed the Wonder Candy worldwide fifteen years ago, things just took off."

"Was I ever here in the future?" asked Buttersample?

"Yes and no," answered Edward. "You disappeared twenty-five years ago, so no. But you're here, so yes. Do you get it?"

"I don't see my family...my wife, and kids, and my folks," said Henry. "Are they...?"

"I'm afraid so." Edward sadly shook his head. Henry bent down and started to cry. "Oh not that, Candy Man," smiled Edward. "I fired them. You know, sent them on their way. They're living somewhere, maybe here, maybe Bordertown." Henry sucked in a deeply relieved breath of air.

"Look, this is where I leave you," directed Edward. "You will be the head of our candy operations here. You'll work seven days a week and twelve hours a day. We'll talk about your salary later. Jake, please show this man to his office. He has twenty-five years of catching up to do." Jake led Henry upstairs. Bryan and Caroline watched a defeated Henry disappear as the elevator door closed.

"Onward," charged Edward. "The next stop of the tour will definitely interest you, Professor." Edward, Frake, Stanley, and the kids walked toward the corner of Main and First Streets. They stopped at the corner. The former Spring Valley National Bank had been replaced by a much taller building. It was still a bank, but with a new title… Livingstone National Bank.

Bryan pulled out his video camera and started filming the scenes around him. Edward rolled his eyes. "Please, you want video?" He spoke into a small microphone that was attached to the lapel of his tweed jacket. "Zoom in RoCam five on downtown Main Street and First Street." Within seconds, a camera about the size of a ping pong ball blazed through the air, hovered in front of the group, and then spun past them. "Now that's the technology of the future," bragged Edward.

"Where are all the stores?" questioned Bryan. "You know, like Mr. Drexel's or the department store?"

"Gone, all gone," Edward said with satisfaction. "You can order what you want on your miniature hand-held computer." Edward grabbed his computer out of his coat pocket and showed the kids.

"So then what is all of this?" asked Stanley, referring to all of the skyscrapers and scores of buildings that surrounded them.

Edward smiled a deep, knowing smile. "I'm glad you asked. See that is where you'll fit in here in Livingstonia. This is the Livingstone Science and Space Research Academy."

"But what about the Observatory? The campus?" questioned Greenlee. The group crossed the street and stared at the high-rise buildings that were once the city hall and police station.

"You see, since you never returned to Spring Valley on the day of the time machine launch," explained Edward, "my dear friend, Professor Eric Van Hausen, was ruined. He was booted out of Spring Valley, and the observatory closed. The town suffered and businesses closed. Fifteen years ago, I, along with my comrades Frake and Jake, made the city our own. We saved it."

Edward gazed with pride at the town he had built. "I started building a new observatory, right here," he continued. "We had so many new citizens arrive, we had to build new housing where the park used to be."

"I don't like this Spring Valley at all," whimpered Caroline.

"But none of this would have happened if we could have returned," assured Greenlee.

"Don't you love what the time machine can really do?" gushed Edward. "You two knuckleheads were just trying to move around in time to observe. I used the time machine to make myself a king, a grand success, the vitally important person I was meant to be."

"But why Spring Valley?" challenged Stanley. "You could have chosen any place in the world."

"Why not Spring Valley?" retorted Livingstone. "It was the perfect scenario. I knew the town well. I had the perfect plan."

"You'll never get away with this," avowed Bryan. "My dad and Professor Van Hausen will bring the time machine back and rescue us."

Edward looked down patiently at Bryan and smirked. "I don't think that's going to happen. You see, your dad designed the chip that enabled the time machine to function, and he's here with us now. Get used to this place kid, it's your new home."

"I want my mommy," cried Caroline as she wiped the tears off of her face.

"Your mom should have traveled with you," clucked Edward. "That was the plan. I really had no need for the candy man. I had already obtained his formula." Bryan reached into his pocket. The piece of Wonder Candy was still there. Opening it was supposed to be the result of a safe and happy return home.

"I'm afraid he's correct on this one," said a dejected Professor Greenlee. "I think that we're in a bit of a sticky wicket for a time."

"I love the word time now," blurted Edward. "There was an age where Professor Van Hausen and I worked together for years, perfecting the time machine. All was good, until you showed up with your formulas and your goodie-goodie attitude. Ah, but I harbor no ill will. This is all here because of you."

Stanley paused for a moment. "So what am I and my kids to accomplish here?"

Edward shrugged his shoulders. "You will have a job here in the science department and a new home on the sixth floor of one of our many high-rise apartments. I don't actually have much need for you now that you're here."

"Well, but what will the kids do when I'm at work?" asked Stanley.

"They'll stay home, attending to their studies I suppose. Everything is on computer now for them. There are no schools around here, just my research center campus. That's where everyone in this town works."

"But where is everyone?" Bryan cut in. "I don't see anyone."

"Working," answered Edward. "That's what robots, I mean intellectual human androids do."

Jake rejoined the group. "Shall we boss?" asked Frake.

"Yes, please take them to their new home." Edward's tone became dismissive as he was obviously finished dealing with the travelers. "I have many busy details to attend to. I have to speak to that Sheriff Taylor, the former deputy. I don't think he's a wise choice to remain sheriff anymore. It's time to replace him with one of my units." Edward paused awkwardly. "Well then," he said and abruptly turned and strode off. He called back lightly, "May I never see you again, Professor Greenlee. But you will probably see me, I'm everywhere." His laughter faded with him around the corner.

Frake and Jake escorted the Greenlees to their new home. It was clean, furnished, and move-in ready, but it lacked the warmth of a real home. "I miss Mum," Caroline sniffled.

"I miss her, too." Bryan hugged her. "And Trixie and Seymour. What are we going to do, Dad?"

"We will do what Greenlees do best," directed Stanley resolutely. "We will work hard and not give up. We will get through this sticky situation...and hope that somehow Professor Van Hausen can rescue us."

While the Greenlees contemplated their new life twenty-five years into the not-so-pleasant future, the folks of the real-time Spring Valley awaited the return of the time machine. The hour had almost passed, and all eyes, both nationally and worldwide, were fixed on the science lab, eagerly waiting for the revolutionary device to return.

CHAPTER 14

"THIRTY SECONDS AND COUNTING," CONFIRMED the reporter inside the laboratory, as Professor Van Hausen monitored the controls on his console.

"Thirty seconds and counting!" The Mayor's enthusiasm echoed through loudspeakers all across the campus and across the world. Ralph, Jenny, Elt, and Bernadette watched the screen intensely, while the crowds began to settle and hush.

Van Hausen wiped the sweat off of his brow. He smiled at Mrs. Greenlee and checked his watch. Trixie and Seymour were in the laboratory, waiting for their humans to return.

"Ten...nine...eight...seven...six...five...four...three...two...one!" announced the speaker.

Everyone watched. Nothing happened. The professor scanned the computer screen. The computer acknowledged the time machine's presence, and then suddenly it bleeped off the screen. The professor checked his watch again. He pushed a series of buttons. The professor looked for a clue, but there was nothing. The time machine was off-line.

"Professor, any comments on the return?" asked the reporter.

Van Hausen became nervous, and a bit frazzled. What happened? Why this? Why now? It was just on-line, now it was gone. He had no clue. "Uh, we were tracking them until a few seconds ago," replied Van Hausen tensely. "I'm sure it's just a glitch. We should get them back any second. If I could just locate them, we'll be right on schedule."

Mrs. Greenlee anxiously laid her head into her hands. Her eyes began to tear, but she remained calm. Her husband was a scientist; he would make sure that he and the kids would be okay. Trixie watched her human. She could sense that something wasn't right, but didn't know what it was. Where were her younger humans?

Fifteen minutes later, the crowds began to get restless. Angry shouts of "Where are they?" and "What is this, a joke?" unnerved the Mayor and his staff. Officials and more reporters attempted to enter the lab, for they had their own questions ready for Professor Van Hausen.

After an hour had passed and there was no sign of the time machine, Professor Van Hausen decided to speak to the crowds, both outside and on television. Mrs. Buttersample and her children were allowed to enter the laboratory and wait beside Mrs. Greenlee.

The professor greeted the crowd with an explanation and an apology. "...And I assure you all that we're doing our best to bring Professor Greenlee, his children, and Mr. Buttersample back safely," he told the crowd. As soon as he was finished, Van Hausen and a couple of his aides fled to the lab and began to re-trace their steps from the launch. Hopefully a clue would lead them to some answers.

Ralph's dad, along with Wendy Rodgers, had remained at the stage area. They both agreed that they would wait a little while longer, but soon they would have to go home. There would be live coverage of the event, so if there was a change, they could view it on television.

Ralph felt helpless. His friends were in trouble. He wanted to do something, but what? Ralph, like everyone else, had no idea where the time machine was. How could he help? How could he travel to the future without a time machine? Ralph wondered if in some way, Elt might be able to help.

When it was time to leave, Jenny asked her mom if Ralph and Elt could stay with them. They could take the dogs for a short walk, and watch TV for any breaking news. Mr. Eltison agreed, so the kids and their pets rode home together with Wendy Rodgers.

Inside the car, Bernadette stayed close to Elt, sitting next to him and in between Ralph and Jenny. This was the first time since the thwarted bank robbery that Elt and Berndatte had sat so closely together, and Bernadette was still waiting to hear about Elt's mission to outer space. She also wanted to discuss the current situation. But with the humans so close, they couldn't talk about anything.

By the time they arrived at the Rodgers' home, Ralph decided that he had to take some kind of action to help his friends. He wasn't sure what to do, but he knew he needed to help. He had an idea, but had no clue if it was going to work.

Jenny walked inside for a few minutes, so Ralph made his move. He bent down, twisted Elt's collar, and stared at the stone. Was that a button or not? He pushed it. The stone began to glow on and off. He watched the stone pulse for about thirty seconds. When Jenny returned outside, Ralph released Elt's collar.

"Hey, whatcha doing?" asked Jenny.

"Oh nothing," returned Ralph. "I thought I saw something on Ralph's fur, but it was just a piece of grass or something."

Jenny paused for a few seconds. "You think Bryan and Caroline are safe?"

"I don't know," answered Ralph glumly.

"Maybe they're stuck somewhere, like in deep space."

"Maybe. I don't know," replied Ralph.

Jenny pressed her lips together. "Let's not talk about that anymore. Let's go for walk while my mom fixes dinner. Maybe we can help her when we get back." Ralph nodded.

Ms. Rodgers prepared a delectable meal; chicken, mashed potatoes, and a salad. The meal was perfect, but the kids ate very little. Jenny wanted the television on, just in case the time machine returned.

Elt and Bernadette wandered over to the dining room, sat down, and finally whispered together quietly.

"What's going on?" asked Bernadette.

"I don't understand," confessed Elt. "What were we watching on that big human picture machine?"

"All I know is that Trixie's humans went on some kind of trip," stated Bernadette.

"Without their pets?" questioned Elt. "I usually go on trips everywhere with my humans."

"This was different. Did you watch the picture? I think they just disappeared, and never came back."

"I believe my human sent for help," Elt informed Bernadette.

"What do you mean?"

"The Trianthians replaced my stone. This one has new features, like maybe it will help me fly. My human pushed on it. Now maybe they will help us." Bernadette peered over and sniffed at Elt's collar. She couldn't see anything, but believed Elt this time.

Ralph suddenly noticed that it was getting dark. "I better go home, Ms. Rodgers," said Ralph. "Thank you for dinner."

Jenny sat up. She had been lying on the couch. "Call me if you hear anything."

"I'll probably be watching the TV just like you," said Ralph.

Ralph and Elt hurried home before darkness fell. The boy showered and changed into his pajamas, while Elt found a space to rest under the dining room table. Mr. Eltison changed channels endlessly, searching for any updates, but there was still no sign of the time machine. The cameras depicted a defeated, baffled Professor Van Hausen. There were so many questions. Everyone could see that he held no answers. Sheriff Thomas and Deputy Taylor were at the campus, answering questions and attempting to assist.

"Still no news," reported Mr. Eltison as Ralph walked into the living room. "Did you and Jenny know anything about the time machine?"

Ralph shook his head no. "Bryan and Caroline just said that they were going to ride in it with their dad and Mr. Buttersample. That was it."

Mr. Eltison turned back to the news with great interest. Professor Van Hausen was being interviewed. "Evidently, the professor tested the machine himself three times with no problems."

Ralph shuffled away. "Good night Dad, I'm going to bed."

"Good night Ralph," called his dad. "I'm sure everything is going to turn out fine."

Ralph flopped down on his bed and tried to go to sleep, but kept tossing and turning. He thought about Bryan and Caroline. He wondered if they were scared. Finally, he shut his eyes and dozed off.

Elt knew that his human was upset. Something was definitely wrong. He plodded into the darkness of Ralph's room to check on his human. Jumping up onto the bed, Elt wondered if Trixie and Seymour knew what was happening. He settled at the foot of the bed and started to doze off. But just then he heard a voice on his transmitter.

"Elt, Elt, can you hear me?" Elt opened his eyes, but was still in a sleepy daze. "Elt, this is Matheun. Am I coming in loud and clear?"

Elt awakened fully. He quietly rose out of bed, sneaked through the hallway, and peered out to see if Mr. Eltison was still seated in his recliner in the living room. Ralph's dad was there, but had fallen asleep. Elt rushed through the kitchen and darted out of the doggie door. Finally he was free to say, "Yes, yes this is Elt."

"Did you set off the alarm on your stone?" asked Matheun.

"No, it was my human," answered Elt.

"What is happening?" insisted Matheun. "Are you under attack? Is it the Quadrasones?"

"No. Let me wake up my human." As quietly as he could, Elt raced back into Ralph's room, licked the boy on his face about a dozen times, and after nudging him from the bed, led him past a sleeping Mr. Eltison. Ralph opened the kitchen door and stepped onto the back porch.

Matheun's voice was adjusted to speak to Ralph. "Greetings, is this Elt's human?"

"Coladeus, is that you?" inquired Ralph. Ralph twisted Elt's collar.

"No, this is Matheun, the First Officer on board Trianthius I," reported Matheun. "Why did you push Elt's alarm?"

As quickly and thoroughly as a ten year-old could in the middle of the night, Ralph explained the dilemma involving the missing travelers and the time machine. "A time portal transporter?" asked Matheun. "Very advanced for your species, I must say." Matheun summoned his captain and soon Coladeus was able to communicate with Ralph.

"We will be orbiting your planet shortly," assured Coladeus.

"What can I do?" asked Ralph.

"We need Elt to gather some of the Earth friends he worked with on his earlier mission, the bank robbery," explained Coladeus. "I'm afraid recruiting help from other planetary systems may take too long."

"But your space pod only holds two," said Ralph.

"Please have Elt and his team join us at the landing site," directed Coladeus. "Where we met on the night of Elt's mission."

"Can I come with them?" begged Ralph. "You're gonna need a human."

Coladeus paused. "This could be a very dangerous mission," he warned. "And, if we don't return you back this night, there will be trouble when your parental human wakes up."

Ralph was determined. He pleaded his case to the Trianthian leader. "You're gonna need a human to communicate with any other humans we meet in the future. I'm not sure if aliens..., uh sorry..., will be accepted in the future."

"Well, that's a good point," confirmed Coladeus. "Please meet Elt and his mission team in the same area as before. I will speak to Elt now." He spoke to Elt in Canine and in a flash, Elt scorched through his yard and was gone.

Thoughts raced through Ralph's mind. "I have to get dressed!" he realized. Ralph tip-toed back inside, passed his sleeping father, and quickly changed his clothes. In mere minutes, he was outside, waiting by Elt's doghouse.

Meanwhile, Elt belted out a few warning barks, hoping to draw some urgent attention. Jasmine was the first to appear by his side.

"What's going on?" she wondered.

"We're going on a mission," declared Elt. "Meet me in my backyard." Then he zipped away.

"Okay! I'll just make my way over then," said a confused but interested Jasmine.

Chin heard Elt's warning and was standing at his front gate. He didn't ask questions, but received instructions from Elt before dashing off for Elt's yard.

Bernadette was asleep under her dining room table. Luckily, she hadn't slept with Jenny that night, for her human was asleep on the couch with the news still broadcasting live from the observatory. Bernadette's ears popped up when she heard her friend's bark. She rushed outside. "What is it?" she asked.

"We have to save those humans," commanded Elt. "You want to know where I went on the mission, come with me."

Bernadette never looked back. Elt opened the gate and she scurried through to meet him.

Juan and Max couldn't be reached, for they were inside. They never heard the warning barks or couldn't convince their humans to let them outside in time. Sarge had just stepped outside for a short walk. Mr. Davis had let his Boxer out, and then sat back down, glued to the television coverage of the launch. Once he heard the message from Elt, Sarge was out of his gate and on his way.

Ralph soon heard footsteps entering the backyard. He couldn't believe his eyes. Jasmine the cat was followed by Chin, Sarge, along with Elt and Bernadette. The pets gathered around Ralph. They all stood silent, watching each other. Ralph gazed upward, waiting for the pod to be visible.

Suddenly, in the blink of an eye, Chin, Sarge, and Jasmine dematerialized, and were gone. "Whoa, what just happened?" Ralph asked out loud. He stood frozen. Did the pets just get zapped or something? Seconds later, Ralph felt a rushing emptiness as he, Elt and Bernadette disappeared too.

CHAPTER 15

RALPH OPENED HIS EYES. HE glanced over to his right. Elt was there, staring at him. The room was faintly lit, with isolated glowing areas produced by the beings that resembled Coladeus.

Ralph had often daydreamed of participating in a real live mission with both Elt and the Trianthians, but it all happened so fast, he was still stunned. He was standing in his backyard one minute, the next he was, well who knew where he was?

A green-glowing Trianthian escorted Ralph, Elt, and Bernadette away from the transport modules. A door hummed and they entered a room, much smaller than the briefing room Elt and Sparky had met in. The other pets were already there. Bernadette nudged her way next to Elt. Ralph's mind was still in disbelief mode. He wiped his eyes, expecting to awaken from a dream.

"You must be Elt's human, Ralph," The strong voice came from behind the boy. Ralph spun around. There was a Trianthian in front of him, but it wasn't Coladeus. This one resembled a younger version of the Trianthian leader. The alien strode a little closer and stopped right in front of the boy and Elt.

"I'm Matheun," the first officer introduced himself. He held out his four-fingered hand. Ralph was hesitant, but then shook hands with the alien. "I trust you enjoyed our new method of transportation?"

"It wasn't what I expected, but I liked it," remarked Ralph. "There's no ride like that in any amusement park I've been to before."

Matheun smiled. "Follow me. The captain is waiting for you."

Ralph, Elt, and the rest of the neighborhood pets followed. Sarge, Jasmine, and Chin were basically in mild shock. Elt had spoken previously of beings from outer space, and they remembered the super dog speaking with them at the old warehouse, but this was the real thing!

The group fit tightly in the ship's elevator. Chin sniffed the air while Jasmine jumped on Elt's back to conserve room. There was a strange silence, but no one expected the canines or feline to be the first to communicate with the aliens.

"Do you guys have a time machine or something?" Ralph finally inquired.

"No," answered Matheun tweaking his distransulator.

The elevator slowed to a stop. When the door whooshed open, Matheun stepped out and signaled for another Trianthian to take his place inside. "Ralph, may I please have you and Elt accompany me to the captain's chair?" asked Matheun. Ralph eased out and motioned for Elt to follow. The other pets watched the doors close in front of them. Inside the elevator, Sarge lost all of his patience.

"Does anyone know what is going on here? I go outside to take care of some personal business. The next thing I know, I'm surrounded by these...I don't know what they are."

"I know what's going on," said Bernadette calmly. "We're on a mission to rescue Trixie's and Seymour's humans."

"But where are we?" meowed Jasmine as she stretched her legs and searched for something to scratch her front paws on. "Did we do that thing like I saw the other night?"

"Yep," barked Bernadette softly.

Sarge was frustrated, and a bit anxious. "I want to be back home, with my humans. And my dog biscuits."

"You did say yes to Elt when he asked?" questioned Bernadette.

"I didn't know we were going to get dog-napped and sent to this place," complained Sarge.

"I wonder what they're talking about." Jasmine purred.

"Hopefully a plan to rescue the humans," envisioned Bernadette.

"Ah, wise plants make fruitful outcome," commented Chin. The group had almost forgotten that he was there.

"That's plans, not plants," blurted Sarge.

The elevator door opened. The pets were escorted into the briefing room. A plan was being established by the Trianthians to assist Ralph in rescuing the Greenlees and Henry Buttersample.

At the same time, on the Captain's Bridge, Ralph and Elt approached Coladeus, seated in his chair. There was something noticeably different about the Trianthian elder. He seemed distant; deep in thought. His glow wasn't as bright as it usually was. Ralph sensed something was wrong, but didn't know what.

"Greetings, Ralph," welcomed Coladeus. "What is happening in Spring Valley?" Matheun slid over to his computer screen. Ralph, who had dreamed of moments like these, was almost too nervous to talk now that he was on board Trianthius I and face-to-face with Coladeus. He glanced down at Elt, who wagged his tail and nudged Ralph forward with his snout. Ralph stepped closer to the Trianthian.

"Well, my friends, Bryan and Caroline, their dad is like a, well he is a professor," began Ralph. "He and this other professor built a time machine. Earlier today, they took a trip to Spring Valley twenty-five years into the future. But they didn't come back when they were supposed to. Now no one knows how to get them back."

"Interesting," commented Coladeus. He gazed over at Matheun, who had begun scanning his computer screen upon hearing Ralph's explanation.

"He's accurate in his statement," reported Matheun. "I'm afraid that the news of this time displacement mechanism has eluded us. This is the first time that my scanners have reported it."

Coladeus slowly rose from his chair. Ralph could tell that the Trianthian was moving slower than he had before.

"I am very impressed," announced Coladeus. "I, well, I mean we didn't realize that earthlings had conducted experiments in such an advanced technology as time travel."

Ralph cleared his throat. "Mathuen told me you don't own a time machine."

"He's correct," answered Coladeus. "But we did invent one some time ago."

"Did it work?" questioned the boy hopefully.

"Yes, it did," replied Coladeus. "In fact, I journeyed through time myself."

"So, what happened to it then?" asked Ralph.

Coladeus smiled. "We destroyed it."

Ralph was surprised by Coladeus's response. "Why did you do that?"

"You see Ralph," started Coladeus, "our species learned long ago that time travel can cause many problems. Just one tiny interaction or change can alter the present, or the past."

"But how can we rescue them if we don't have a time machine?" Ralph interrupted.

Coladeus paused, and then shifted his attention over to his first officer. "I have him on screen now sir," stated Matheun. Coladeus waited for an image to pop up on the big screen before them. "Ralph, we are contacting our most intelligent scientist, Mogulus. Hopefully he will find an answer to our query. He does believe in a theory of time travel without the use of a time machine."

Ralph and Elt watched as an image appeared on the screen. Mogulus resembled a normal Trianthian, but a much older one. He possessed wiry, white hair and was clad in a long burgundy robe. Mogulus was Trianthius' master scientist. He had invented the distransulator, the re-generation chamber, and most recently, the transport modules. If anyone knew how to solve this dilemma of rescuing the time travelers, Mogulus would be the one.

Coladeus updated Mogulus on the current situation. He explained that there were six beings from Earth, one human and five pets, on board Trianthius I, ready to somehow travel to the future and rescue the group. Mogulus spoke to Coladeus in their alien dialect. They also conferred with Matheun, who monitored his computer screen intermittently. The scientist repeatedly swiped his tele-screen.

Ralph and Elt watched the Trianthians converse. Mogulus reached for his distransulator while Coladeus turned back to speak with the group from Earth. "I believe Mogulus has strategized a plan to rescue your friends," he announced.

"Really? How?" asked Ralph, his eyes shining. He and Elt edged their way closer to the Trianthian.

Mogulus gazed directly at the group. His eyes, although squinted, were wise and caring. "In theory, it is said that one can travel into the future or the past by completing multitudes of rotations around the medium involved. In this case, that medium is your planet Earth."

Coladeus continued, "So we will send Trianthius I around Earth at incredible speeds. If we complete it correctly, we will arrive at the desired moment in time."

"With precise calculations of course," added Matheun.

"It's our only hope at this time," concluded Coladeus.

"I don't want to relate the odds of this theory working in our favor," Mogulus hesitated. "I'm sending Mathuen the calculations that I have composed right now." But unexpectedly, the resolution on the screen began to dissipate, and soon Mogulus' signal was lost.

"It must be some type of signal interference," explained Matheun as he attempted to restore the scientist's image. "I did receive his calculations."

"So it appears, we have one chance to rescue these time travelers," stated Coladeus.

"And one chance to return," added Matheun.

"Our engines...can they support the speeds required to complete the mission?" asked Coladeus.

"It can be done," answered the first officer. "But there is a high degree of risk. If Mogulus's theory is incorrect, we could be frozen in some portal of time forever."

"Or just get really dizzy," offered Ralph.

Coladeus read the desperation and the hope in the expressions of Ralph and Elt. "We're here always to assist civilizations in need. If we don't attempt to save these humans, time as we know it on Earth will be forever altered." Coladeus eased back into his seat. "Ralph, you and Elt will join the others in the briefing room."

Ralph nodded. "Come on boy, let's go see the others." Ralph and Elt followed a crew member into the elevator. The elevator whooshed closed and whisked them towards the briefing room.

Coladeus turned off his distransulator. He directed Matheun to forward Mogulus's calculations into the ship's navigational system. The ship's computer would then calculate the correct number of revolutions and the speed it would take to travel twenty-five years into the future. He briefed his crew on what was about to take place, and then motioned for Matheun to initiate the mission.

Trianthius I began its expedition around Earth. Attempting to stay beyond the planet's satellite tracking systems, the ship's velocity reached light speed. Trianthius I raced forward faster, faster, and faster.

Ralph, Elt, and the rest of the neighborhood pets were seated in the briefing room. Ralph was the only one actually sitting in a chair, while the canines and Jasmine sat on the floor. As the ship began its whirlwind journey, two Trianthians entered the room and hastily sat down beside Ralph.

The growing speed of the ship's revolutions caused increasing centrifugal force that pressed them all toward the floor. Faster and faster they spun. Soon a screeching roar emerged that intensified as the speed increased. The dogs began to bark and whimper. Jasmine belted out a few loud meows. "What in the world is happening to us?" barked Sarge. "I think my face is falling off!"

"Elt, what's happening?" pleaded Bernadette.

"I don't know," shouted Elt. "But I think we're traveling to where Trixie's humans are."

Ralph began to shake nervously. He couldn't believe this was happening. Was this just a bizarre dream? He had wanted adventure. He had craved space travel. But this was not what he had bargained for. He felt like he was spinning in an extreme amusement park ride, but worse. He wondered if Trianthius I would ever stop.

Ralph felt the wall behind him begin to shudder, and suddenly the set of metal shelves directly above Ralph's head clattered themselves right off the wall. Ralph attempted to duck out of the way, but the force was just too powerful. At that moment, out of nowhere, a streaking Elt flashed above him and caught the heavy apparatus head-on. Elt lowered the unit to the floor and braced it against the wall where it couldn't threaten anyone. Ralph exhaled, amazed and grateful.

Chin was the only one who remained calm throughout the entire ordeal, even with all of the shaking. The spaceship spiked to the speed of light and the revolutions seemed endless. There were flashes and clamors emanating from the spaceship's engines. Did Trianthius I burn all of its resources to venture into the future?

Finally, finally, the ship began to decrease its speed. The room slowed its spinning and eventually came to a rest. Everyone in the briefing room remained still with the exception of the two Trianthians, who stood up easily and walked out of the room.

Elt scooched over to Ralph to make sure that his human wasn't harmed. Ralph buried his face in his fur. Bernadette scanned the room. She spotted Sarge, Chin, Jasmine, Elt, and Ralph. Everyone seemed fine.

"So, are we there?" barked Bernadette.

"Don't know," woofed Elt.

CHAPTER 16

"Ship's status?" asked Coladeus.

Matheun scanned his computer. He zipped through the ship's database and energy level monitors. "All systems are in full operation."

"Good. And can we sustain a trip back? That is, if we are indeed twenty-five years into future Earth?"

"According to Trianthius I's data, we have enough power to return back to the present and arrive on Trianthius," confirmed the first officer.

Coladeus watched the screen before him. There was Earth, plain as day, but what day was it? "Do we have any confirmation?"

Matheun diligently scanned the readings. "I believe Mogulus's formula to be correct. We should be twenty five Earth years into the future."

Coladeus stood. His legs were weary, but not just from the trip. There was something definitely wrong. "You know you're getting older when you have to double your visits to the re-generation chamber." He slowly walked over to Matheun's computer to catch a glimpse of the first officer's discovery.

"We must be quick," directed Coladeus.

"I will take care of it sir."

"Try to minimize your presence."

"Certainly," assured Matheun. "I don't think humans, even twenty-five years into the future, would be ready for us."

With a dismissal from his captain, Matheun headed down to the briefing room to brief the troops for the next mission, probably the most bizarre endeavor the Trianthians had ever participated in.

Elt had finally relaxed when he realized the trips around Earth were over. Things seemed normal again. Then the door hummed and Matheun entered, adjusting his distransulator.

Matheun shared the Trianthian plan with the pets first. Sarge had one question; when could they go home? But he never really asked it. He wanted to help rescue Trixie's humans, just as much as he wanted to go home.

Matheun recalculated his language device to English and explained the strategy to Ralph. "I'm going to accompany you on the trip." Ralph nodded, reassured. "You and Elt are going to lead the mission, however," continued Matheun, "I need to avoid human contact. Are you ready?"

Ralph was nervous, yet excited. He inhaled deeply, swallowed, and let the air out abruptly. "Let's do this."

The first officer led Ralph, Elt, and the neighborhood pets to the transport modules. The same two Trianthians that accompanied Ralph in the briefing room handed Matheun a mini-sized computer tablet, about the size of a small paperback book. One of the crew members also handed him a couple of recently charged Trianthian stones. Matheun held onto the tablet, and placed the stones in his pouch.

Ralph and Bernadette entered the small modules first, while Chin and Sarge walked into the larger two. "We will be right behind you," affirmed Matheun. "We have located a wooded area in future Spring Valley where your natural wooded recreational facilities are located. According to my scanners, it appears that the time displacement device,...that's your time machine...is located in this area." Matheun looked to his shipmate manning the module controls. "Engage," he commanded. The teammates vanished.

Ralph blinked his eyes. All he had felt this time was a tingling sensation, almost the same sensation as drinking from a new soda can. Bernadette wagged her tail when she noticed Ralph by her side. Sarge and Chin accompanied Ralph as he ventured out slowly past a stretch of trees. He noticed a lake in the distance, but nothing looked familiar. No one was visible in the immediate area. Nightfall was approaching.

Ralph heard a sudden slight humming behind him. When he peered through the branches of a spruce tree, he breathed a sigh of relief. Matheun, Elt, and Jasmine were materializing right before his eyes. Jasmine quickly hid under a set of low-lying bushes. Elt sped over to Ralph and Bernadette. Matheun began entering notations on his tablet.

"Is this really Spring Valley?" inquired Ralph.

Matheun viewed the landscape before him. "Yes, but from what I remember of our last mission, many changes have occurred in your living zone."

At that moment, something caught Ralph's eye, an object standing alone in a clearing just beyond a stand of pines. "It's the time machine!" exclaimed Ralph. "They must be here."

The search party rushed over and Matheun inspected the time machine using his tablet. "The time displacement device is missing and the power capability is low, but otherwise the machine seems to be in operational order."

Ralph scratched his head. "What do we do now?"

"I'll stay here and repair the device," instructed Matheun. "You need to find your lost humans and return them here as quickly as possible." Matheun adjusted his distransulator and voiced his instructions to Elt and the other pets. Then he re-adjusted his language device.

"The rather large canine will stay here to watch guard while I repair the unit," Matheun continued. So Chin remained. "Ralph, we must be expedient, for the longer we stay, the lesser the odds of us returning."

Ralph attempted to remember where he was in the park. There wasn't much of a park left, so all he could do was venture in the direction of downtown. The sky darkened. Ralph couldn't believe the sights before him. This was Spring Valley twenty-five years into the future? Ralph and the animals walked past the lake and all of the living quarters, but where was everyone? No one was out walking their pets or enjoying the fresh air.

When the mission team reached Main Street, Ralph didn't know where to begin. There were very tall skyscrapers surrounding him. This place looked more like the picture of New York City that he had discovered when reading a book at the Spring Valley Public Library. Everything was so different. Ralph forced his mind to think. He knew that Buttersample's Candy Emporium should be the first building on the right on Main Street.

"*Livingstone's* Candy *Wonderland*? Who's Livingstone?" Ralph whispered to himself. He approached and pushed on the door, but it was locked. The lights were on inside, but there was no one to be seen. Elt sniffed the door, glanced back at Bernadette, and then abruptly seized the door handle with his mouth. Ralph witnessed Elt's spectacular strength in action for the first time when it really mattered. Evidently, even futuristic doors were still no match for an incredibly super-powered specimen like Elt. Elt didn't tear the door off its hinges. He allowed just enough room for all of the team to enter.

"Let's go!" charged Ralph as they squeezed their way into the store's dark lobby. The factory was on the second floor, so the team scurried up the stairway into the production area. Noises came from the back kitchen. Elt surged ahead of his human with Sarge, Bernadette, and Jasmine following. Elt nudged open the swinging door to discover who was back there.

Elt was astonished to recognize the man he had met not too long ago; Henry Buttersample. Henry was watching his new staff prepare a batch of the Wonder Candy. But something was quite odd about the staff; they were robots, not humans.

"No, no, no," muttered Buttersample. "You have to wait five minutes after the ingredients boil before you add more sugar." Henry heard a noise from the swinging lobby doors. When he looked up, all he could see was a small finger motioning him to draw closer.

"What is the meaning of this, Livingstone?" exclaimed Buttersample. "Checking up on me already?" When Henry opened the door, he couldn't believe his eyes. There were four pets and a young boy? What was going on?

"Mr. Buttersample, I'm Ralph...Ralph Eltison," said the boy. "I'm here...I mean we're here to rescue you."

Buttersample was befuddled. "How did you...Where did...You look so familiar."

"I was there, with my dog Elt, on opening day," shared Ralph.

Henry thought for a few seconds. "Opening day? That was twenty-five years ago. You couldn't possibly..."

"It's hard to explain," Ralph cut in. "We need to get you out of here fast and back to present day Spring Valley."

"Wait a minute," processed Henry. "I do remember you, and your dog, the hero. These must be..."

"They're all heroes sir." Ralph smiled but he was in a hurry. "Are the Greenlees with you?"

"No. I don't know where that madman took them," grumbled Henry.

"Who, Mr. Crum?"

"No, the professor's assistant, Edward Livingstone, who worked at the observatory. I'm afraid he outsmarted both professors. He transformed Spring Valley into his city, and even took over my candy emporium."

Ralph thought for a few seconds. He wanted to get Mr. Buttersample out of there, but he needed to find the others, and fast. "Do you have any ideas at all where they might be?"

The group stepped outside and Henry glanced one way, and then the other. He focused on the skyscrapers down past Main and First Streets, lit with fluorescent blue and green lighting. "This is the way towards the new observatory. Maybe the Greenlees are near there."

"Let's go," charged Ralph.

"Wait," warned Buttersample. "Livingstone has these robots everywhere. Some float around in the sky and record everything for him. You can't just wander around. They're going to know you're here."

Ralph made eye contact with Elt. "What do you think, boy? Can you pick out their scents?" Although Elt didn't fully understand human speak, he instinctively knew exactly what Ralph was asking him. Elt quietly barked to his friends. Sarge began to sniff; Bernadette too. Even Jasmine attempted a few whiffs in the night air.

In less than thirty seconds, Sarge had caught a trace of their scents. He forged ahead with the rest of the group right behind him, including Mr. Buttersample. As they fled, two robot associates exited the candy factory, witnessed the events, and began reporting the events into little microphones attached to their wrists.

The new observatory campus sprawled out about ten acres past the site of the former city hall and police station. The campus, although technically advanced and eye-opening, seemed lifeless, mainly because there was no human life surrounding it.

Elt raced past the site of the old train station. It appeared now to resemble a monorail transportation facility, for rails at least twenty feet high forked out from there in many directions throughout the campus and city. There were no vehicles anywhere to be seen. Elt slowed and waited for the others to catch up. The pets traded glances. "Which way?" he asked.

Sarge sniffed the air. Henry and Ralph, breathing hard, watched as the pets worked their magic. Just then, a RoCam zoomed past, detected the group, and then soared away. Bernadette was the first to move onward, a little slower this time. Elt followed. Sarge continued sniffing, and then he and Jasmine caught up with the others.

In a short time, they reached the middle of the campus. The scent was stronger now. Bernadette stopped at the entrance to a high-rise apartment complex. Once again the front doors were locked, and once again, Elt opened the door with ease. With the scent on everyone's noses now, Elt hastened his pace. Ralph and Henry watched with amazement how quickly the neighborhood pets worked together in solving the unknown whereabouts of the Greenlees.

A robotic security guard peeked around the corner when it heard a noise in the lobby. It spoke in a flat computer voice. "How did you get in here? Stop please."

Elt spotted a door that led to the stairs. Ignoring the guard, he jetted through the door, followed by the rest of the rescue team. Up and up they climbed quickly. When they reached the sixth floor, Elt stopped and sniffed briefly. Bernadette and Sarge, panting heavily, followed suit. Jasmine jumped in between the three dogs.

"They're somewhere close," announced Elt.

"The future smells so different," admitted Sarge. "I hope we're right on this one."

"I smell Tender Vittles," wheezed Jasmine. The canines just stared at her and shook their heads.

"Here goes," motioned Elt as he reached for the door handle and carefully opened the door from the stairway into the hall. Endless doors lined the hallway in both directions. The canines' sniffers were good, but could they find the Greenlees in time?

"If we get back safely, I'm considering hiring these pets to head my "smell division," commented Henry wryly.

"What's that?" wondered Ralph.

"Don't know yet, but I would hire them nevertheless."

Each pet stopped at a different door. "I do believe this is the one," Jasmine spoke with finality.

"No, it's got to be this one," interrupted Bernadette.

"You're both wrong," barked Sarge softly.

"Well we can't just tear down every door," Elt reminded them.

"I'll bet my last bag of feline food that this is the correct door," insisted Jasmine. The pets quieted. They knew she was serious. They all walked away from their claimed door and sat beside her.

Ralph and Henry remained hidden behind the door in the stairway as Elt crept up to the door. "Is this their new home?" called Ralph into the hall. Ralph waited for a vocal response, but what he received was a wag from every pet tail.

Elt scratched at the door. Nothing happened. He scratched it a second time. Then they all heard footsteps on the other side of the door. Were they at the right place?

The door opened. Elt's eyes widened. Bernadette drew closer to Elt. Sarge opened his mouth and stared at the door. "Well I'll be a monkey's uncle," he whispered. Jasmine leaped onto the Boxer's back.

Standing at the door was Bryan Greenlee. Confused, he glanced back into the room, and then returned his attention to the group of pets. "Hello, what's going on? How did you get...?" The realization began to dawn on Bryan.

"Who is it son?" asked Professor Greenlee from the room inside.

Caroline appeared at the door. "Daddy! It's Elt and Bernadette!"

Professor Greenlee rushed to the door. "What do you mean, kids?"

The professor leaned his head into the hallway, noticing Sarge the Boxer. "Wait a minute, that's the old fella that lives across the street."

"And that's the kitty cat that lives near us," added Caroline.

Ralph and Henry moved into the hallway where the Greenlees could see them. "The animals are here to rescue us," explained Henry.

"But I thought we were in the future," Bryan questioned.

"Right now I don't know," answered Professor Greenlee.

"I don't really think we're in the future, Daddy!" Caroline squealed. "Ralph is here, too. And he still looks the same."

"How did you all get here?" Bryan wanted to know.

"Never mind that right now," answered Ralph. "We have to leave now!"

Professor Greenlee hesitated. "This could be one of Livingstone's tricks. Where are we going?"

"Back to the time machine," replied Ralph. "There's someone working on it right now...I hope."

Henry grabbed the professor by the arm. "Professor, you must believe him. I do. But we need to go now."

"Daddy, let's go home, our real home," begged Caroline.

The professor exhaled, then nodded in agreement. Leaving everything behind, the humans rushed after Elt and the rest of the neighborhood pets down the stairs. When they reached the lobby, Elt swung the door open so hard that it nearly tore off its hinges.

The security robot had called in for reinforcements, and they were gathering in the lobby when Elt and the others busted in and dashed out of the doors. "Halt! Go no further!" directed the computer voice.

Elt nudged Caroline to jump on his back, and then they bolted ahead of the others. "Wow, he's like a race horse, that one," remarked Professor Greenlee as he watched Elt run.

The group galloped down Main Street, past the new bank and then the candy factory. The security robots, led by Fred and Zeb, were hot at their heels. Night had fallen, and it was difficult to determine just how many robots were giving chase.

With Elt in the lead, the pets and humans passed the lake and forged ahead to the park. The lights in the park were scarce, but Elt and the other canines followed their sprinting noses to the area where

Matheun, Chin, and the time machine should have been. But then the canines sensed something else; a new danger.

Elt skidded to a halt first, with the others following suit. Three flashlights clicked on and shone into their faces. There, standing in front of the time machine were Edward, Frake, and Jake.

"Leaving so soon?" chuckled Edward. The group shielded their eyes and could only get glimpses of the vile men. "Who is this group, Professor, and how did they know how to locate you?"

Caroline slid off of Elt. Ralph edged his way forward, closer to his dog. "I'm Ralph Eltison, and I live in Spring Valley," he announced bravely. "Just this morning...I think..., I watched my friends, their dad, and Mr. Buttersample leave on the time machine. When they didn't return, well, we found a way to rescue them."

"Impossible. Preposterous!" declared Edward. Frake and Jake laughed along with Edward.

"Well, no, it's actually true," announced a new voice from behind a set of bushes. It was Matheun. His glow was weaker than usual, but still green enough to cause heads to turn.

"By golly, it's a little green man," exhaled Bryan.

"You're an alien!" exclaimed Professor Greenlee.

"And you are a very observant human," returned Matheun.

Edward couldn't believe his eyes. He swallowed hard. In all of his planning, scheming, and vision, he never imagined a rescue squad appearing in less than a day, and without the use of the time machine! How did they get here? Who was that green guy? And how in the world did they find his "guests"?

Zeb and Fred, along with all of the security robots, had come up and encircled the group, equaling four solid rings of robots. Ralph and the others were completely surrounded. There was no escape. Edward breathed a little easier. "Frake, Jake, apprehend these miscreants," he commanded with disgust.

The two men approached Ralph, Elt, and the others. Instantly, the new threat, along with the familiar ugly scent of Frake and Jake, inspired Elt and his friends. Elt charged forward and growled. The others imitated their leader.

The two brothers couldn't believe it! How could it be? Not these dogs and cat again! Instead of an attack, there was more of a retreat. Frake and Jake began to run, but Elt leaped forward and secured Frake by his britches.

"Time to bite another butt," barked Sarge as he chased Jake. Before he knew it, Jake had two dogs and a cat on top of him.

"Seize them!" yelled Edward to the crowd of robots around him. Fred, Zeb, and the robots surged towards the humans. Since Elt was busy with Frake, Ralph had to think of something fast. Chin suddenly darted out of the bushes. He stopped in front of Ralph and growled. Then Ralph spotted Matheun.

"You better watch out!" shouted Ralph. "Or this alien will melt you all into jelly!"

Matheun instantly caught on to Ralph's strategy and stepped forward. "That's right! In fact, I'll turn you into a...a..."

"He'll turn you into a peanut butter and jelly sandwich!" finished Caroline.

Zeb and Fred looked at each other. That sounded serious. They began to back away, and the robots followed.

"Incredible," cried Professor Greenlee.

"Unbelievable!" boasted Henry.

Edward knew that he had no more allies. He acted quickly. Before the dogs could catch him, he jumped into the time machine, reached into his pocket, and began to insert the chip he had retrieved earlier. But then he noticed a new chip already in its place. He turned the machine on. It started to spin. Faster, faster, and faster.

Elt started to release his hold on Frake, but it was too late. Even his exceptional strength wouldn't slow down the time machine's revolutions. The robots, along with Zeb and Fred, had hastened their retreat. After a sizeable puff of steam, blinding flash and boom, the time machine disappeared. The group was alone and the only sound was low growling in the direction of Frake and Jake. Five humans, four dogs, two captives, one cat, and an alien, were stranded in the park, twenty-five years into a future that no one wanted.

CHAPTER 17

"WHAT ARE WE GOING TO do?" worried Ralph. "He just took the time machine!"

Professor Greenlee seemed unconcerned with the situation they were facing. He was totally mesmerized by Matheun's appearance. The alien first officer began to chuckle. "I think that the situation will improve in the next of Earth's thirty seconds."

"How is that alien communicating with us?" Professor Greenlee's mouth hung slightly open.

"It's that thing he wears around his neck," informed Ralph. "He can communicate with almost any being in space."

Matheun spoke up. "I think it's about time."

Sure enough, the wind began to swirl and bright flashes of light flickered quickly across the area. Steam began to form. Ralph and his friends hurriedly backed away from where time machine once stood. When the steam cleared, there it was, the time machine returned! But it was empty!

"Where did that man go?" asked Bryan. Everyone, with the exception of Elt and Sarge, who were still securing Frake and Jake, came closer to the device.

"I anticipated the human's reaction," remarked Matheun. "I re-programmed the coordinates. In such haste to escape, the human didn't realize where he was actually traveling to. I set the time machine to return in five Earth minutes."

"But where did Edward go?" inquired Ralph.

"Somewhere, in very deep space," responded the Trianthian. "I suppose he stepped out, for he is no longer here. We must hurry before those droids determine that I won't transform them into...peanut...something..."

"Peanut butter and jelly sandwiches," laughed Caroline.

"The time machine only holds four travelers old boy," informed Professor Greenlee. "I'm afraid we have five, plus all of the pets."

"And what do we do with those two?" asked Henry, referring to Frake and Jake. "Our not-so-good friend Edward brought these two cronies with him from the past, but still in the future for us, I guess." Henry briefly explained to Mathuen how Edward retrieved Frake and Jake, and then transported them to where they were now.

"We must deliver these two 'cronies' as you say, back to the same exact spot just before the time he retrieved them," instructed the Trianthian. "Does the time displacement device contain a record of its travels?"

"Absolutely," answered Stanley with a bit of pride. "I still can't believe I'm communicating with an intellectual space alien. Brilliantly fascinating!"

The professor scanned the records of the time machine's recent departures and arrivals. "Just what I suspected," reported Stanley. "Edward erased the records of most of his trips into the future, probably to keep them hidden from us. Luckily, he didn't erase his trip to pick up these lads."

The professor noticed the two green, glowing stones attached to the power transformer. "What are those doing here?"

"They will be your power source," replied Matheun. "They should supply the necessary power to return you and your comrades home. I had to make some adjustments."

Elt and Sarge dragged the two brothers on board the time machine. The men strapped themselves in while Elt crept into his seat. Sarge jumped off and joined the others on the grass. Professor Greenlee pushed a series of buttons, strapped himself in, and soon the time machine began to spin again. In less than a minute, the time machine had disappeared with a boom, flash and a cloud of smoke.

"They'll come back for us, right?" asked Ralph, concerned. Matheun smiled and walked away from the others. "How will *you* return back to the past?" Ralph wondered.

"The same way we traveled here I am hoping. We need to reach Trianthius. Coladeus, he is not..." Matheun didn't finish the thought.

Ralph felt a lump in his throat. "He'll be okay, won't he?"

"We are all not feeling like ourselves," replied Mathuen. The transmission with Mogulus was our last successful communication with Trianthius. I fear something has gone terribly wrong."

Bryan and Caroline ran to the alien and hugged him. "Thank you for rescuing us," Bryan said gratefully. Matheun smiled at them, then touched the screen on his hand-held tablet and within seconds, he vanished.

"Amazing," whispered Henry Buttersample.

"Where did the green man go?" cried Caroline.

"Back to his spaceship, the Trianthius I," Ralph answered gently.

The group was suddenly interrupted by the noisy, steamy arrival of the time machine. They spread out quickly, giving plenty of space and waiting for the flashes and steam to dissipate. Professor Greenlee and Elt were seated inside. "Let's go home," declared Professor Greenlee.

"That's a grand idea!" Henry grinned. "But how will we all fit?"

"We'll have to do our best," answered Stanley.

Henry climbed into one of the rear seats, while Caroline and Bryan shared the other. Ralph and Elt sat together next to the professor, while Sarge, Bernadette, Chin, and Jasmine squeezed in wherever they could.

"Wait a minute," announced Bryan. "I want to celebrate our rescue."

Bryan reached into his pocket and snatched his piece of Wonder Candy. He unwrapped the candy's shiny, silver lining and plopped the candy into his mouth.

"Me too!" exclaimed Caroline.

"Not the way I imagined it, but now is as good a time as ever," agreed Henry. He reached into his pocket and handed both Ralph and the professor a piece. "Happy travels."

"Let's eat them together! Caroline squealed. "Ready? ...one, two, three, go!"

Caroline, Ralph, Henry, and Stanley unraveled the paper and dropped the candy into their mouths. Each expression was priceless. Ralph's piece started sour; Caroline's sweet, Bryan's chewy, Henry's crunchy, and Stanley's chocolaty.

"Out of this world!" gushed Ralph as he chewed and sucked on his candy. "What kind of candy is this?"

"Wonder Candy!" shouted Caroline and Bryan.

Ralph glanced at Elt. "Boy, if you were allowed to eat candy, I would definitely give you a bite."

Professor Greenlee smiled. "Are you ready children and pets?"

"Ready!" cried the kids. Sarge and Bernadette barked. Jasmine meowed. Chin smiled.

The professor reset the coordinates. The Greenlee kids found spare masks under one of the rear seats and dispersed them to every human. The professor set his mask to the side. Greenlee clicked a few buttons and soon the time machine began its familiar spin, although slower than usual.

"I'll have to make some adjustments, for we are carrying too much weight," warned Greenlee. "Hold on everyone!"

The professor pressed a couple more buttons, and then turned the dial on the power meter to maximum. Never before on any of its previous voyages had they needed to use everything the machine had, but Greenlee knew they were going to need it.

The time machine began to increase its revolution speed. Elt watched Bernadette, who was nestled between Professor Greenlee and Ralph. The noise and the flashes frightened her. Elt reached over and laid a paw on her back. She turned and licked his paw.

Ralph closed his eyes for a few seconds. When he opened them, he could see Earth through the window. Bryan and Caroline scanned the scene before them. Compared to their initial trip, this one was rockier, far less smooth, unsettling. Caroline heard a noise below her. Then she threw off her mask.

"It's breaking apart!" she screamed. Indeed, a five inch crack ⅃ developed on the rear side of the time machine. Professor Greenlʮ glanced back, noticed the crack, and then read his scanner.

"Hold on everyone!" he shouted.

The crack ripped another inch.

"We need something to bond it together!" bellowed Henry. At that moment, a brilliant thought came to him. He lifted his mask and nabbed the piece of Wonder Candy, which had transformed into a flavorful piece of bubble gum, out of his mouth. Caroline and Bryan watched while Henry jammed, jabbed and spread the miraculous gum into the crack. Hurriedly, they snatched out their own candies and handed them to Henry. Ralph yanked off his mask, stretched back and donated his gum too. The Candy Man molded and pushed until the crack was filled. He sat back then, and they all watched and waited, holding their breath for a long moment. Nothing happened. The crack remained stable. The bonding powers of the Wonder Candy had worked! The crack was sealed.

"There ya go!" exclaimed Bryan.

But then a red light on the time machine console began to flash and a loud buzz startled them all. The pressure gauge was rising steadily under the current conditions. Professor Greenlee turned his head around and shouted, "When we land, we need to get out fast!"

*   *   *

The laboratory was quiet. Professor Van Hausen was there alone. The television cameras had moved outside, still broadcasting live, making news out of none. The professor had given up hope, for his screen scanned nothing; the time machine was off-line and there were no signs of it returning.

Henry's family had joined Mrs. Greenlee and the pets in the office next to the lab. Henry's children played with Trixie and Seymour, but their hearts weren't in it. Mrs. Greenlee meditated, praying for her family to come home safely.

Professor Van Hausen's career had gone from brilliant to ruin in one short day. But he wasn't thinking about his career, his life-long dream, or his missing time machine. He was filled with despair because his partner, Professor Greenlee, the children, and Henry Buttersample, were all missing, too.

Van Hausen laid his head on the desk near the control console. He closed his eyes. His head throbbed. He had tried to retrieve the time machine, but it hadn't responded. What happened?

An alarm suddenly sounded on the control console. Van Hausen sat up abruptly. Lights began flashing. The beeping sound and flashing lights meant only one thing...

"It's..." said the professor incredulously. "It's coming, it's here!" No one heard him. The door to the office next door was closed.

In an instant, the platform began to spin. Broad beams of light blazed throughout the room. Van Hausen watched intensely. Something didn't feel right. He checked his controls. Another warning light flashed and buzzed. The time machine was overloaded and overheating! And then a deafening roar erupted.

The professor had to react quickly. He flipped a few switches and adjusted some dials on the console. Steam poured into the laboratory. Hearing the noise next door, Mrs. Greenlee ran out of the office, but before she reached the lab's doors, the machine had arrived.

When the haziness cleared, there it was, spinning more and more slowly, and there they were, looking frantic, fumbling with their seatbelts. Professor Van Hausen stared. The beleaguered time machine carried the four familiar travelers, plus a handful of pets stuffed into every available space.

Greenlee shouted, "Everyone get out! She's going to blow!" He turned around and unsnapped Bryan's buckle, pushing him out the door with the tangled scramble of Chin, Sarge and Jasmine. Caroline's belt wasn't so cooperative. Professor Greenlee reached to free her, but it was stuck fast, pinning Caroline to her seat.

"I'm stuck Daddy!" she screamed, crying.

"I know, pumpkin," her father tried to soothe her. "We'll get you out." Henry, now unbuckled, joined in the attempt to free Caroline.

Chin, Sarge, and Jasmine zoomed out the laboratory doors, and sped down the hall. But Bernadette stood frozen near the front seats. The whole scenario was just too frightening. Ralph had unfastened his belt, only to realize that his shoelace had caught underneath his seat. He couldn't free himself either.

"Stupid shoelace!" blurted Ralph. "Just let me go!"

Black acrid smoke curled up from the underbelly of the time machine. Time was running out! Inside the machine, Elt realized he had only seconds to react, but so many to save: Ralph and Caroline and his canine best friend, who stood motionless, in trouble. With lightning speed, Elt sprang into action, lurching over the seat and clamping his teeth into Caroline's belt. It snapped! The professor and Henry grabbed her and pushed each other out. Flames burst out of the transformer.

"We must leave now!" shouted Van Hausen. He hastily steered the others toward the laboratory doors, shoving the children in front.

Meanwhile, Elt flashed back over to Ralph, tore off his shoe, and seized the boy by his shirt. Ralph, sensing Elt needed an extra hand or mouth, scooped Bernadette securely. Instinctively, knowing time was gone, Elt leaped. What happened next, the three would remember forever. Whether it was the new stone, or Elt's determination to rescue Bernadette and Ralph, no one would ever know, but Elt the super dog achieved his dream; he flew. Elt soared towards the lab's fifteen foot ceiling. Then it happened. The time machine exploded, sending a shockwave of sound, light, and debris all the way outside. The force of the explosion thrust Elt and his rescued ones violently toward the ceiling, but then a large piece of debris shot past them, tearing a hole through the ceiling right in front of them. At the last possible moment, Elt leaned toward the opening and the dark, black sky beyond it.

Van Hausen, the Greenlees, and Henry Buttersample had been hurrying toward the exit, but they didn't make it in time. Mrs. Greenlee was just reaching to open the doors for them, when the explosion forced her back into the hallway. The professors and Henry shielded the kids from the blast, but the force of the explosion knocked all three of them unconscious.

Ralph couldn't believe it. His dog, his super dog, had just saved his and Bernadette's lives. And he did it by flying! Elt couldn't believe it either, but there he was, high above the laboratory, soaring to safety, and with no one seeing them. All eyes and ears were on the explosion in the lab.

Bernadette began to recover. Realizing Elt had just saved her life, something changed in the way she looked at him. Something strange, but wonderful. Elt sensed the same thing, too. They weren't just friends anymore.

Elt looked for a place outside of the chaos to land and then spotted Chin, Sarge, and Jasmine in a nearby field. The two dogs and cat watched in amazement as Elt, still holding Ralph and Bernadette in his mouth, landed before them.

"He did it, he finally did it!" gasped Jasmine. After a brief moment of shared joy, the animals hurried away, for Elt and the others knew that they were far away and had to return home before daybreak. With amazement, Ralph watched how Elt and his friends jumped onto the back of a flatbed truck, which had stopped to check out the events at the laboratory.

Elt and Bernadette sat close together the whole ride home. For Elt, there was no more affection for Trixie. The next time they'd meet, there would be no more staring, no more mesmerized glances. Something had changed during the mission. He realized that his true love was beside him all the time, his best canine friend. They had experienced danger together now more than once, but this time, something was different. The pups were maturing.

When the truck stopped at a traffic light one block from the corner of Schoolhouse and Valleydale Roads, everyone jumped off. It was time to return home.

*   *   *

The security team, reporters, and camera technicians scurried into the laboratory. Stanley and Henry were lying on the floor, beside Caroline and Bryan. Professor Van Hausen rose, wiped his face with his hand, and then struggled through the debris to reach his travelers.

"Daddy!" exclaimed Caroline.

Professor Greenlee's eyebrows twitched. He moved slightly and tried to open his eyes. At that point, Mrs. Greenlee, Trixie, Seymour, and the Buttersample family poured into the laboratory, pushing past the reporters and security personnel. They knelt down to comfort the travelers.

When Professor Greenlee finally opened his eyes, he lifted his hand and rubbed the back of his head. A flying object caused by the explosion must have hit him square on. Mrs. Greenlee hugged her husband, and then her children. Trixie jumped on Caroline and started to lick her face endlessly. Seymour rubbed up against Bryan's arm.

Henry's family woke the groggy candy entrepreneur. The explosion had rattled him, too.

"Professor Van Hausen, what just happened?" asked the reporter.

Van Hausen rushed over to Professor Greenlee. "Stanley, thank goodness you're all alive and well. What happened? How did you get back?"

There were more questions, but all Stanley could do was rub his head. "Honestly, I don't know how we returned...I can't seem to remember clearly. It all seems like a dream. For some reason, though, I feel that we should re-direct our efforts here on campus and study... alien life."

Henry couldn't remember much either. Ralph, Elt and his friends, Edward, Matheun...they were all just partial memories, and he couldn't arrange them to make sense. But who would have believed it anyway?

The fire and rescue teams entered the laboratory. The professors, Henry, and the children were examined by the emergency personnel.

Suddenly, Trixie put her nose in the air and took a whiff. Even through the smoke, fire, and debris, she picked up a scent; something that was familiar. She scanned the area, but couldn't see who she thought she smelled.

*   *   *

Ralph's dad awakened early the next morning. He had slept all night on his recliner. When he finished rubbing his eyes, he noticed the news was still on the television. At the bottom of the screen flashed the caption: FOUR TIME TRAVELERS RETURN UNHARMED – TIME MACHINE EXPLODES!

Mr. Eltison couldn't believe it. He walked into the kitchen and found the newspaper on his chair, just like it always was. He opened the paper to the headline announcing the time machine's disappearance. Their return must have occurred after the newspaper had been printed.

Mr. Eltison entered Ralph's bedroom. His boy was sound asleep. "Ralph, Ralph wake up." Ralph uttered a series of nonsensical chatter, and then fell back into his slumber. "Your friends returned safely," continued Ralph's dad.

"That's great," mumbled Ralph.

Mr. Eltison smiled. He glanced over at Elt who was resting, but with his eyes open. Elt began to wag his tail. Mr. Eltison patted Elt's head, and then headed to the kitchen to brew a cup of coffee.

Jenny's mom attempted to wake her daughter. Jenny had fallen asleep on the couch, watching the news the night before. Bernadette had crept outside just after she had fallen asleep. Now the Cocker Spaniel slept at the edge of the couch.

Sarge collapsed onto his back porch and scratched at the back door with his right paw. Mr. Davis opened the door. Sarge staggered in.

Chin crept into his doghouse earlier that morning and fell asleep. There were none of his famous proverbs spoken. Chin was exhausted. Jasmine fell asleep on her back porch, right next to her water and food bowls.

CHAPTER 18

It was a late August morning when the first day of school arrived. Ralph's dad woke up extra early that morning to fix Ralph pancakes for breakfast. It was a tradition that Mrs. Eltison had celebrated when she was a kid, and it carried forward.

Ralph left a few minutes early so he could stop by Jenny's house. Jenny and Ralph waited for Bryan and Caroline to come outside. "Our first day in an American school," boasted Bryan.

"I can't wait to meet new friends," added Caroline.

After the safe return of the time travelers, Spring Valley once again bore a feeling of jubilance. There were interviews after interviews performed by the local and national media.

Professor Greenlee began to regain partial memory of the whole ordeal, but it was still sketchy. Somewhere, in the vast interiors of his mind, he remembered the kid who lived down the street, a bunch of the neighborhood pets, and an alien, all saving them from Edward Livingstone. But if they were traveling along on the time machine, where did they go after the explosion? It must have been a dream.

The camera that Bryan used to film the future was destroyed by the blast. When Bryan and Caroline were asked questions about the return home, they never mentioned the rescue attempt by their friend and the neighborhood pets, nor the little green man who repaired the time machine. The one big detail they did relate was concerning the futuristic Spring Valley.

"The park wasn't a park anymore. There were bunches of buildings everywhere, and skyscrapers!" related Bryan.

"And don't forget about the robots!" added Caroline. Mayor Helms assured the folks of Spring Valley that there were definitely no plans in the future to erect skyscrapers or destroy the park to make way for houses.

Professor Van Hausen's popularity dwindled some with the failure of the time machine to return promptly and its subsequent explosion. Although he still owned the patents and plans to construct another time machine, and although time travel had been his life's passion, he had no immediate desire to dive back in. "We're going to step out in a new direction of space technology," Van Hausen revealed at a news conference just two days after the launch.

It wasn't quite clear whether Professor Greenlee had any say in that decision, but he knew one thing. He loved his family, and he was elated to be home. He spent a week with them before returning to work. They enjoyed walks in the park, a trip to the pool, and back-to-school shopping at Gletzky's Department Store. He spent the rest of the time at home, working on his house. Painting the kids' rooms involved a couple of trips to the paint counter at Feldman's Hardware. There were no more discussions about time travel in the Greenlee home.

Henry Buttersample was also excited to be reunited with his family. It was "business as usual" for the candy man. After a short nap, Henry strolled downstairs to his candy wonderland, greeted everyone with glee and worked his usual shift with relish. His recollections during interviews were the same as Stanley Greenlee's. He too, had received a hard hit to the head during the blast. He wasn't sure if any of it was real.

As for the Wonder Candy, Henry decided not to distribute his product just yet. He wasn't sure why. It just didn't feel like the right time. There was no denying it though; the Wonder Candy was deliciously genius, and incredibly strong, durable enough to hold a time machine together. Maybe one day down the road, Henry would market his invention to the world.

Concerning Edward P. Livingstone, both Stanley and Henry related their encounter with Edward to Professor Van Hausen. The discrepancy in usage hours on the time machine would have confirmed their story, but the time machine was decimated, of course. The hour meter was never located. Professor Van Hausen made sure that Edward's belongings were kept safe in his apartment on campus. Just maybe, although very doubtful, his old friend would return. Edward himself was never seen or heard from again.

When the kids reached Spring Valley Elementary School, they split up and found their respective classes. Ralph, Jenny, and Bryan reported to Mr. Campbell's fifth grade class. Caroline trekked over to her third grade class with Mrs. Walker.

Sam Meyers shuffled into Mr. Campbell's classroom. The whole ordeal with Elt and Ralph still weighed heavily on his mind. In fact, it may have changed the former bully's demeanor. Sam was the first fifth grader to welcome Bryan Greenlee.

On the walk home from school, the kids passed by an abundance of the neighborhood's pets. Juan sat on his front porch and yelped. "Buenos Dias," he barked. "I wish I could have gone on the trip with you." Jasmine had shared the news of the rescue with him.

Max watched the kids walk by while he was inside, enjoying the cool comfort of the air conditioning. Mrs. Petrie's front picture window allowed the Sheepdog plenty of room to oversee outside events.

Sarge barked at the group for a few seconds. Ralph stopped in front of the gate, dug for the wrapped remainder of his sandwich from lunch, and handed it to Sarge. The Boxer enthusiastically accepted.

Ralph ran across the street and met his friends in front of Jenny's house. "Are we all gonna walk later?"

"After we finish our homework," answered Bryan.

"Five o'clock then?" inquired Jenny.

The kids nodded yes. Jenny opened her gate and disappeared through the side door. Ralph turned to head home, but Bryan and Caroline timidly stopped him. Ralph was puzzled. Caroline nodded to her brother. He returned the gesture.

Caroline finally turned to Ralph. "We know your secret," she whispered. Bryan smiled.

"Secret?" asked Ralph.

"We remember," stated Bryan. "You, Elt, the other pets...you rescued us. Well, you and the alien."

Ralph didn't know what to say.

"How did you do it?" asked Caroline. "How did you disappear when the time machine exploded?"

Ralph suddenly got nervous. "Have you told anyone?"

"Not a soul," answered Bryan.

"We can't tell anyone, not even Jenny," warned Ralph seriously.

Bryan and Caroline nodded, smiled, and ran off. "Mum's the word," Bryan called. "See you at five."

Ralph headed home. He spotted Chin, who had just stuck his head out of the doghouse. Their eyes met. Chin yawned and crept back inside.

Jasmine ran along her fence line as Ralph approached his yard. He stopped to caress the back of her neck, bringing out her peaceful purr. "The secrets you must know," he chuckled. Then he straightened and noticed Prince outside in his yard. The Doberman barked a couple of times, and then resumed his patrols around Mr. Dawkins' yard. Ralph finally approached his own backyard.

Before his first round of fifth grade homework, Ralph play-wrestled with his dog on the living room floor. He found the red ball and threw it down the hall. Elt kept his pace at normal and returned the ball to his human.

After homework and a snack, Ralph asked his dad if he could meet his friends at five. Mr. Eltison approved, so Ralph and Elt ventured to Jenny's house. Jenny and Bernadette were outside waiting for them.

"Hey, Bernadette is going to the vet's office this weekend," reported Jenny.

"What for, shots?" questioned Ralph. Bernadette leaped off the porch to join Elt. The two sat together on the grass.

"Maybe, but I think my mom mentioned she's going to receive a computer chip," replied Jenny. "You know, if Bernadette is ever lost again, then any vet can find us with the help of the chip."

"That's a good idea," commended Ralph. "I think I should talk to my dad about that for Elt."

Jenny bent down to pet both Elt and Bernadette. "You know what we've been thinking about?"

"What?" asked Ralph.

"Mom and I were thinking about allowing Bernadette to have one litter of puppies," Jenny gleamed.

"Wow, that's kind of cool," remarked Ralph.

"We'll see," said Jenny. "Mom and I think it would be cool too, you know, before..."

"Before what?" asked Ralph.

Jenny giggled. "You know, before she goes to the vet and can't have any more puppies."

Ralph paused for a few seconds. "Oh, yeah."

There were times when Ralph and Jenny still walked their dogs together, but a new neighborhood tradition had begun. Bryan and Caroline, along with Trixie and Seymour, joined the group for as many walks as they could. Even Seymour wore a leash. He was more eager to walk with Caroline, while Bryan usually held Trixie's reins.

A new walking tradition meant new walking routes; the group ventured past Spring Road into an adjoining Valleydale neighborhood. But the walks still usually ended at Jenny's house, where the kids would gratefully receive glasses of lemonade and the pets an enormous bowl of water.

Where Elt was concerned, Trixie's beauty had lost its potency. Elt and Bernadette were inseparable. Their friendship had blossomed into something wonderful and innocent...love.

Trixie could see it. In vain, she attempted a few of her tricks to try and woo Elt's affections, but Trixie wasn't too upset about the situation. There were rumors spinning around the neighborhood pet circle that Trixie had received several late night visits from Prince, although those rumors were never confirmed.

After dinner, Ralph played with Elt outside until it was dark. They stared at the stars, hoping a triangular, green one would appear. Ralph no longer wondered what it was like to travel in space. He had been there, though no one would believe him. Caroline and Bryan remembered Ralph rescuing them, but they had no idea how their friend had found them. They never asked.

Although Ralph and Elt couldn't talk to each other directly, the same subject was on their minds. Was Coladeus going to be alright? Were the Trianthians able to return to the present? Would they ever hear from the friendly aliens again? Ralph wondered if they would ever partake in a mission again.

Since he had school the next morning, Ralph knew he couldn't stay up late. Elt followed his human inside. After a quick shower, Ralph spent a few minutes on his dad's computer. He googled the song *Bernadette*, by the Four Tops. Clicking his fingers to the beat, Ralph listened to the entire song.

Afterward, Ralph crawled into his bed. Elt followed and found a comfy spot to lie in. "How about a bath when I get home tomorrow boy?" asked Ralph. Elt wagged his tail, wiggled up to Ralph, and began to lick his face. Elt hugged his dog, and then twisted the collar once again. The stone shimmered with its greenish glow.

What a wacky and wonderful summer it had been. Elt and the neighborhood pets had gone missing, and then showed up and stopped a bank robbery. He was approached by real aliens on several occasions. The Candy Emporium had opened its doors, and Spring Valley had become famous for time travel. Ralph himself had assisted in an important space mission and had actually traveled through space and time. Soon it would be Elt's birthday, even though Ralph didn't know the exact day Elt was born. Then Ralph would turn eleven. Ralph closed his eyes and dreamed of more space adventures.

Later that evening, when Ralph had fallen into a deep slumber, Elt sneaked outside and met Bernadette in her backyard. The two sat together and stared at the night sky. Elt nudged his head against Bernadette's. She laid her head up against his. All was tranquil in the Valleydale subdivision. Hopefully things would remain peaceful for a while. The summer had been a busy one for Elt and his friends.

But suddenly a strange, scratchy and garbled noise interrupted the silence of the evening. Elt knew immediately what it was. A message was transmitting through the stone on his collar.

"Elt, Elt, can you read me?" The voice sounded familiar. "This is Sparky." Elt's ears perked up, but the message kept fading in and out. "Dude, this is Sparky," repeated the voice.

"Who's Sparky?" whispered Bernadette.

Elt paused. "An old friend." Then louder he answered, "I can read you, Sparky." A long, static-filled pause made Elt think the Golden Retriever hadn't heard him.

"There's trouble on Trianthius!" announced Sparky, suddenly loud and clear. "We're on our way to pick you up!"

Elt and Bernadette stared at each other. And then at the same moment, they grinned and turned their attention to the evening sky, watching for the arrival of the newest adventure.

Coming in 2015 .....
Trouble on Trianthius.
eltsadventures.com

ABOUT THE AUTHOR

Dan grew up in Newport News, VA and attended Virginia Polytechnic Institute and State University. He has devoted nearly thirty years to the motion picture exhibition industry. He currently is employed with Lowe's Home Improvement.

Dan has enjoyed writing all of his life. He has written numerous screenplays, one which was pitched to a major movie studio in 2003.

When Dan was ten, he wrote a story dedicated to his childhood dog "Trixie." Years later that story inspired him to create "The Adventures of ELT the Super Dog." "ELT And The Time Machine" is Dan's second novel and sequel to his first.

Dan now resides in Frederick, Md. He is married and has three sons. The family enjoys their five cats and two dogs.

CPSIA information can be obtained at www.ICGtesting.com
Printed in the USA
BVOW07s2141091214

378705BV00002B/117/P